I0548736

And Then There Were None

By: Clay Thomas Williams

Publishers note

The Cataloging in Publication data is on file at Library of Congress.

ISBN: Soft Cover 978-0615999531

Published by Up Next Media Group

Printed in the USA

Graphics by AMB Branding

Contact Info: upnextmg@gmail.com

Acknowledgments

I told myself I wasn't going to do acknowledgments in the novel due to the fact that I may miss someone, but how could I not? So if I forget to acknowledge you, please charge it to my head, not my heart.

First and foremost, thank you Lord from whom all blessings flow.

To my Mother Maxine (Peachy) Samuels, who like everyone else's mom told me there is nothing I can't do. She is my biggest fan, loudest cheerleader, and biggest supporter. She is truly a little biased when it comes to me. She thinks all my work is great, thanks mom, you're right! I'm still a big baby to this day, if I feel sick, I'll climb right in the bed with my mom. Her prayers and love get me through.

To team Te', my reason for everything, I live to make you proud; Shanique Deleure, Tishaunda Ollivanza, Nicole Renee, Josiah Emanuel, Rion Olivia Mackenzie, and Ava Marie, you are the best. I couldn't have asked God for better children. You guys make me laugh, make me cry, give me drive, and keep me on my toes. Endless hugs when I need them and headaches when I don't, but love me always. J. Star

Daddy (Caswell Elliott) thanks for being there for me. Worrying about me when I'm worrying about you, Cat, I'll talk.

My nana, Ollie Allen, I miss you so much. We talked about this project and she gave me advice that shocked me, but was so on point and so right. Most times, I should have listened. She didn't always tell me what I wanted to hear, but always told me and gave me what I needed.

I would like to thank Andre 'Songmaster' Brown for introducing me to Tanya Robinson.

Just as it seemed all this work was just going to be stored up in my computer and never reach an audience. I got an instant message on the book.

"Girl, call me!

Conversation with Tanya Robinson: Hey, I started Up Next Media Group Publishing, and I want you as my first Author. I read your manuscript and I want to publish it.

Me: Where do I sign up?

Tanya: I got you!

And she does, and Tanya, I got your back too.

You keep your word, you do as you say, and I'm blessed to know you. It's true; God puts people in each other's lives for a reason. I've known you for over 15 years, and no matter how we met or through whom, girl, we're good.

Loyalty and honesty is something you don't see much of.

Thank you, for believing in my work.

To all of my Yvette's': thanks you for the inspiration and the memories, and most of all, the writing material.

Clay (2014)

Table of Contents

Chapter 1

"Good afternoon American Airline passengers. This is your captain speaking; we're currently flying into Montego Bay Airport. The weather here is one hundred andone degrees and clear. Please return your tray tables and seats back to their upright positions, and please take note of our no smoking and seat belt signs. Thank you for your cooperation and have a great day!"

Damn! Finally, after a five hour flight, a dull movie, a quick nap and five glasses of complimentary champagne, I still have a killer headache. The last thing I should be doing on my period is going on vacation; well at least this should be my last day. I'll take a couple of Advil and I'll be okay in no time.

I can't wait to see my baby! He's already here on business and he should be waiting for me at the gate. I only brought carry-on luggage with me thankfully, so there'll be no need to wait in the long baggage claim line.

The plane taxied to the terminal and the flight attendant bid us goodbye. As I walked off the plane with my luggage, you could hear the music from the drums and the singing, welcoming us to Jamaica. The heat here is almost unbearable and it's not helping my headache at all. Looking through a sea of smiles, I see waiting family, friends, and lovers but not mine.

I didn't see him, I walk into the airport and have him paged. I guess I was being a little impatient. I thought to myself, *it's hotter than Hell here.*

I heard his name being called over the intercom, "Mr. Lynwood Rose, would you please meet your party at the customer service desk."

As I turned around to look out the window to the sea of taxi cabs, I saw him. My well toasted, lover. The sun did a number on him.

He noticed me just as I was about to call his name, and we both headed to the door as it automatically opened. He grabbed me and held me so tight; he didn't have to say a word, his embrace said he missed me.

"Hi baby," he whispered in my sweat soaked ear.

"Hi," I replied.

"Hi? That's all I get after not seeing me for two weeks?" He said, sounding a bit agitated by my lack of enthusiasm. "Are you all right?"

"I'm sorry baby. I've got a monster headache. I think I had too much loose panty juice on the plane, my period is just going off and the heat here is like whoa."

"Yeah I know, but you'll get used to the heat and I'll get you something for your head when we get to the hotel. I knew you would over do it with the free champagne," he said with a little sheepish grin.

We both laughed because he knows drinking makes my panties a little loose. He must have not paid attention when I said I had a visit from Aunt Flow.

He grabbed my bag from me, "Damn woman, what the hell you got in here?"

"A little bit of everything! Oh, a couple of swim suits, shoes, evening wear, toiletries, and my jacket. It's snowing in New York and very cold."

"I'm not missing that at all," he said as he hailed a cabby to drive us to our hotel. I rolled down the window hoping the breeze from the moving car would cool me off just a bit, but the breeze was so hot.

It's hard to breathe and the air feels thick, but Lynwood hadn't even broken a sweat; not a bead on his brow. He smelled like that sweet familiar scent of Jamaican Rum and cranberry juice.

Although it's cold in New York, I tried to dress to accommodate both climates. I brought a wife beater with a pair of hip hugger khakis that show just a hint of the matching tattoo of a crescent moon Lynwood and I have. He has the top half and I have the bottom. It kind of looks like a banana cut in two.

I packed a couple of thongs and a bra reluctantly. The problem with being big breasted, going without a bra is never an option. I've been considering a breast reduction but I haven't got the nerve, not to mention the fact that my sweetie loves these knockers.

As small as I am, they look awkward. I'm five foot eight and a half inches tall and a size nine, kind of thin for my height with 36DD's and size six feet. Lynn always teases me about falling over from being top heavy with little feet of hundred dollar bills wrapped in a rubber band.

"Here baby, put this in your woman's place." Lynnwood instructed

I don't know what it's for but when a man hands me a bra load of cash the only information I need to know is where I shop.

"Tavia," he said, "I have a surprise for you!" We walked into the lobby.

At the front desk, Lynn asked the concierge for access to the safe.

Lynn put my passport and ID in it because the safe in our room was broken.

"Sure Lynn, no problem," she said.

"Thanks April," he replied.

"Lynn, what happened to Mr. Rose? What's with the informalities?" I questioned.

"Tavia, calm down, I asked her to call me by my first name."

The concierge, April, stared at me with her "Bitch No She Didn't" daggers. I know that look well, because I gave her the same look. She stepped off to the back pointing the way for Lynn and I to go to the safe deposit box.

She seemed to be disappointed that he wasn't alone. He's been in Jamaica a whole two weeks before I got here.

He's a fine ass, distinguished looking black business man all alone on an island full of women; He has chestnut colored eyes, and a caramel complexion. He must have looked like lunch to a starving hostage.

He stands about six two with a smile that can light up the darkest of nights. Lynn has a way with me I can't explain, I'll go to the ends of the earth for that man. Well to the ends of Jamaica, anyway.

We put all of our important papers, ID and all my jewelry, except my wedding ring in the safe and headed to our room.

April handed me a light blue wrist band to wear around. "All inclusive huh, yes, I'll put this on for you," she said with a thick Jamaican accent.

"Thank you."

"You're welcome, Tavia, is it?" she questioned.

"Yes, it's Tavia, but I'm a tad bit more formal than Lynn."

"Tav, cut it out," he said as he kissed me on my neck and lightly patted my backside. He always looks at me as if I'm the only woman in the world and I loved that.

April, the concierge cut her eyes at me, as if to say BITCH!

"Have a good day," I gloated and walked towards the elevator with a juvenile "Aha, he's my man" look on my face. I know it was petty, but what the hell.

"Hold up, you said you needed something for your headache, I'll be right back."

Lynn took a slow jog to the gift shop and was back within minutes, aspirin in hand..

***

We took the elevator to the eighth floor and when he opened the door; I noticed a bottle of champagne with a couple dozen roses on the table that was made up beautifully for two.

We were in a two story suite; the walls were painted in a soft mauve. The sea foam living room had a cute love seat with an air conditioner directly over it. Our suite had an upstairs balcony and a downstairs balcony outside of the dining area that over looked miles and miles of paradise. Our master bedroom was made for a queen with a king size bed. It was damn near poetic, and it was beautiful, my baby went all out. If I wasn't so hot, I could appreciate this more.

"Sweetie, where is the bathroom? Let me wash some of this day off of me."

"You passed it coming in near the front door," he answered.

Damn, even the bathroom is beautiful. He had my bath drawn before I got here with glow in the dark bubbles and scented rose petals by candle light and a glass of champagne. Nice. The last thing I need is another glass of loose panty juice. I'm also hoping the bath doesn't give me a glow in the dark, floral scented, yeast infection.

I really don't do the bath thing too often for that reason. I'll make an exception today because he went through so much trouble, I'll just bathe with a tampon in.

***

It's amazing what a difference an Advil and a nice warm bath can make. I sat on the love seat, still damp with a mixture of floral scented bath water and perspiration. My towel was half wrapped around me, completely exposing one of my breasts, as the other, peeked from behind the towel.

I gazed through the balcony doors to the beach below just as the island sun was setting on Montego Bay. Lynwood was sitting next to me, running his fingers through my neatly braided hair.

"How's your head?" He asked.

"It's feeling much better, my father always said a head this size is supposed to hurt at least once a week. Besides I think these braids are too tight."

"I don't know why you wear them anyway, you have long pretty hair." Lynnwood complimented me.

"Yeah, thanks to *Dark and Lovely*, baby, if I didn't have these braids I wouldn't be able to do a damn thing to my head with the heat scorching my scalp. I'd sweat my perm out in seconds, and I would have to avoid the ocean, like a gremlin avoids water."

My grandmother is Black Foot Indian and Jewish, my grandfather is Cherokee Indian and African but they all look alike, and have that so called 'good hair.'

Unlike everyone else in my family that gene just didn't get to me and my twin sister. We are like the black sheep of the family, while the rest of my relatives look white, or damn near, with the thin lips and thin hair. A couple of them even have blue eyes and blond hair. Not me and my sister. We're dark caramel with very full lips and slanted eyes like our father. We look a lot like our father and nothing like my mother, who often said if she hadn't given birth to us, she would doubt we were hers. The only thing my mother and I have in common is a slit between our legs. My mother's a beautiful sweet woman inside and out, although I'm always teasing her about her white woman's lips, she says she always wishes she had mine.

In my family my twin sister Yvette and I stand out like a sore thumb. We never had hang ups about it, I love everything about me, down to my hair, that's nappier than a sheep's ass in heat. Without a perm it will shrivel up to my scalp, like a Brillo pad if you wet it. When you perm it, it's pretty as hell. I don't know how women go Au Natural; a relaxer is a God sent gift.

"Lynn, can you turn that air conditioner on?"

Lynn reached over my head to switch the A/C on and I noticed the television was on and playing Good Times. This was the most dramatic, most memorable episode, I could remember. James died; Florida and I said it together Damn, Damn, Damn.

"Tav, you watch too much television."

"And you must have grown up under a rock if you don't know this episode," I said as we laughed. I pointed out without a perm my head would look like Florida Evans.

"Whoa keep the perm," he said playfully as he pinched my exposed nipple and ran his hand down the trail my open towel left, straight to that sweet little spot below my navel.

"You've got pretty hair here and you can't perm that."

"Yea, strange isn't it?"

Lynn moved his head to where his hand was and inhaled. "Hmmm, smells like flowers," he said of my neatly cropped pubics. He moved his nose back and forth over my sensitive spots, letting his hands roam over my breast, around to my hips, pulling me closer to his face with one movement. His lips moved up to my stomach, right under my belly button, and off to my hip. I closed my eyes and lay my head back just enjoying the feel of him touching me, when I felt his thumb hit my clitoris with a soft stroke; I nearly jumped off the sofa.

"What's this?" he asked, referring to the string hanging out of the spot he was definitely trying to get into.

"I told you Aunt Flow was visiting."

"And I told you, I'll run a red light! How heavy is it?"

"Not that heavy, I said it's the last day, the tampon is just in case."

Just when I think Lynn would yield at a yellow light, I felt his hands on my steering wheel as he put the pedal to the metal, twirling his finger around the string, dangling between us, and gave it a yank. The shock of it made me squeal like a pig, it felt kind of funny but it turned me on. Butterflies filled my stomach and I began to shake as if it was the first time.

Lynn looked up at me from between my cocoa brown thighs to catch the look on my face as I damn near erupted.

"Slow down speedy," I murmured in a soft whisper.

"Who's driving this?" He boasted as he became really familiar with the handling of this vehicle. His mouth blew warm breath on my sensitive spot, as his tongue worked circles around my clit, while his fingers were sliding in and out of me.

I begged him to stop, but not really wanting him to. When I did have enough, I reached down and pulled him to me face to face. I nibbled his lip, as I planted Eskimo kisses on his nose.

"Are you ready for me?" He whispered as if someone else was in the room and would hear.

"Show me," I echoed whispering, mimicking his tone.

"Show you what, baby," he asked as his hand guided his male member like a heat seeking missile.

I can't catch my breath. He enters me. I manage to gasp a few words between long deep strokes and bellowed, "Show me how much you missed me."

With each thrust he licked or sucked me from my lips down my neck to my breast. "Lynn, Oh God!" I screamed out as tears welled in my eyes.

Pleasure is a funny thing because with every thrust I felt guilty for feeling good but couldn't wait for the next wave of orgasm to reach me.

"Your skin is on fire."

"Fire from lust," I explained, but he already knew every part of my body was trembling.

My back arched and my legs got stiff, my private area turned spastic and began to pulsate around him. I felt cool water trickle down my face and then an ice chip landed on Lynn's back and quickly melted from his body heat. Ice chip after ice chip landed on us and quickly melted, frequent and sporadic just like my orgasms, soft to hard just like our love making. The glass on the balcony doors began to fog as the frost built up on the front of the air conditioner that seemed to have gone haywire spitting ice chips about the room. We found ourselves running and ducking for cover.

We lay on the floor alongside the sofa laughing and out of breath. I turned on my side feeling a bit nostalgic giving him my backside when I felt him gently tap me on my ass, with his nine inch third leg. My lover is revved up and at the wheel again.

"Turn over on your stomach." Lynn demanded.

I did as I was told with no questions asked. I eased my bottom in the air, putting my feet in between his legs to prevent my legs from buckling from the thrust. There was nothing like a little back shot.

Lynn pushed his hand down on the back of my neck so my bottom would be high and my top low to the bed. He put himself back inside me slow inch by chocolate inch until I fully accommodated him. I never understood how a woman's vaginal area is about six or seven inches in depth from coochie lips to the uterus; how it's possible to manage a lover that is clearly eight or nine inches in length. It's amazing how we stretch to fit.

My lover goes slowly but deeper time and time again, until my hands reach to pull threads from the plush hotel carpet. I lean up so my back is firmly pressed against Lynn's chest. He has one hand around my waist, as the other ventures up around my throat; the firm pressure from his damp hands force my body into convulsions. "Oh God, oh Lynn, oh baby, oh Lynn, oh shit, Lynn." As his mouth and tongue suck the back side of my neck I want to collapse but that grip around my waist and neck is holding me up.

By now, everyone on this side of the island must know Lynn's name and that God was being summoned. I know I'm a bit of a screamer but it turns Lynn on.

"Stay right there," he requested as I felt him positioning himself to knock on the back door.

"Wait!" I squealed like a scared school girl, "What are you doing?" I asked the question as if I didn't know that he was preparing to enter my ass.

"Shhhhhhhhh, it won't hurt, I promise."

"I can't, I'm not ready for that." I told him.

"I'll get you there," he insisted, still on his mission to enter me from behind.

"Lynn no, really I can't." I knew he was stunned at my persistent no, being that I've never denied him anything.

"Come on Tav, you promised when we got to Jamaica."

"I know I promised but I can't right now my body's not ready."

"Aiight," he said sounding like a disappointed child who just found out the Santa myth was a fraud.

"You mad?"

"Nah," he answered, trying not to sound angry.

"So why so quiet?" I pressed the issue.

"I'm just tired, I'm going to sleep."

Why was he so tired all of a sudden? Was it because I slammed the brakes on his rear end collision?

Men and their reverse psychology, I guess he felt that if he showed a little attitude, I'd give in.

Nope, not tonight!

AND THEN THERE WERE NONE

A few minutes go by and he's snoring, just like a man to cum and then go. I lay there, looking at the ceiling, thinking, just how short this time alone with him is going to be. I should really make the best of it. It's not often we have one another to ourselves.

When I get back to the States, I have a soundtrack to finish and I've got a severe case of writers block. Music usually comes so natural to me, but lately it's like I can't get it together. Maybe I'm too happy, I can't think of any heartbreak songs to write, no inspiration. Lynn was always good to me, so I really couldn't complain too much.

I snuggled up next to him on the floor, wrapping my leg over his thigh and placing my braided head on his arm, thanking God for another day and a safe arrival. I kissed Lynn on his well shaven jaw and whispered goodnight. He snorted like a pig in response. He made a loud exhale while repositioning his body trying to get a comfortable spot and drifted off again.

***

Six a.m. and the Jamaica sun was shining on my face through the balcony doors. My body was a little stiff from lying on the floor all night. I'm not as young as I used to be. I get up earlier than Lynn to wash up and brush my teeth and take a shit, which they think we never do.

The things we women do, to not turn a man off; even lose an extra hour of sleep. Just so that we can primp and look and smell exactly like he remembered you before he dirtied you up the night before. Add a little makeup, and a little something to your hair while he's still sound asleep and they think you wake up beautiful.

I slid on my black two piece thong swimsuit with the skirt like tie around my waist as I stood on the upper balcony drinking a cold glass of orange juice admiring the scenery. When Lynn walked up, he wrapped his arms around my waist and kissed me on my cheek.

"Good, Good, Good morning," he bellowed as he exhaled and took in the morning air.

"Good morning, love of my life, how'd you sleep?"

"Like a log."

Speaking of logs, his morning wood was poking me in the butt, I reached behind me and gently patted his little man on the head, "Good morning to you too," I giggled.

Lynn laughed the proud laugh of a proud poppa and popped me one quick slap on the ass.

"Heading to the beach early, huh?" he asked.

"Baby, I'm trying to soak up as much of Jamaican sun as I can in these four days."

"Did you have breakfast yet?"

"Not yet, but I'm going to catch the breakfast buffet down by the pool."

"Well, give me a few; I'm going to come down with you."

He turned to go back in the room and I stayed on the balcony. Out of the corner of my eye, I noticed the couple on the balcony below me. He was a blonde haired guy with a hairless chest sitting in the balcony chair with his head back facing me. A slim built, big bobbed blonde crawled between his legs and was giving his early morning hard log a good morning slobbin'.

He had one hand on her head and the other gripping the arm of the lawn chair about to rip it clear off. I couldn't stop watching even after I noticed he saw me watching them.

The girl's head moved furiously up and down up to the tip where she moved her tongue around the head and plunged fast like a deep sea diver making his dick jerk. Her brightly painted pink synthetic tipped nails were clicking together when her hands connected. Her hair was swinging with every dive. She was hungry, and I was loving it almost as much as he was. He pulled her hair up into his hand and into my view, I guess so we both can get a better look at her work.

I wanted to be her cheering section and shout 'do that shit girl', but of course I stayed quiet and enjoyed the show, she was unknowingly putting on for me, with her lovers help. Giving professionals was never the highlight of my day, but watching this girl do her thing, I was inspired. I gotta give it up to white girls; they can suck a grapefruit through a straw and like it.

To them it's just a part of sex; to us it was total disrespect to be asked to do such a God awful thing. If you were asked to do it, you felt disrespected.

Hell, even Lynn has to coerce me to do it, but after watching girlfriend, I have a new view on the subject.

My balcony neighbor was getting vocal, "Yes girl, suck it," he said as his hand forced her head down faster and faster. He got extremely red about the face and neck; his body stiffened as he announced his arrival and never took his eyes off of me. Slowly his body stopped jerking and he let her hair fall as he stroked her head with his right hand.

His left hand wiped the sweat from his forehead. He ran his fingers through his blonde curls as his girlfriend's head was still bobbing but every time she came up his body jerked violently. I guess I can assume she swallowed, her head was nestled up against his thigh and his eyes were still planted on me.

It's only eight thirty in the morning and she's already sucked her lover dry. *Damn she's good*, I thought, *and now I am so freaking turned on.*

Somehow Lynn snuck up on me, breaking my eye contact with my bone dry neighbor; I almost jumped off the balcony. "Whoa, you scared me," I blurted as I rushed him back across the threshold into the room.

"You're enjoying the scenery, huh?"

"Oh yea, the scenery from this balcony is great," I said with a little giggle.

"Are you hot?" Lynn asked.

"Huh," I uttered feeling like he caught me.

"Are you hot," he asked again. "You don't seem to be complaining about the heat now."

"No, I'm not hot, you were right," I replied. It's funny I hadn't even thought about the heat.

"Told you you'd get use to the heat, you ready to go?"

"Yup," I replied as I took one last peek over the balcony, but my view was gone.

Chapter 2

After a pool side breakfast, Lynn remembered a phone call he had to make.

"I'll meet you at the beach." I told him.

"You sure you want to go alone?" he asked as he took a sip of his orange juice.

"I'm a big girl daddy; I think I'll hit the beach topless," I snickered just to see what his reaction would be.

"T-T- Topless!" he stuttered choking on his last sip of OJ. "Topless," he repeated. "Are you serious?"

"Why not? White woman do it all the time! Besides, I don't know anybody here, and I am quite sure they're never going to see me again. When on vacation, you can pull shit you would never do at home."

"Got a point, but I don't believe you'll do it." I wasn't really going do it, but it sounded to me like he was calling my bluff.

"You know I'm daring," I exclaimed as I turned to walk away, removing my skirt like a wrap, revealing the thong swim bottoms I was wearing.

Lynn barked at the site of my bare naked bottom with the black string traveling straight up my ass. "Whoa, whoa, whoa, where you going in that?"

"To the beach." I responded, never missing a step. Lynn shook his head in total disbelief and mouthed 'I love you."

"I know!" I shouted waving my hand goodbye and never turning around.

"I'll be back in about a half."

"Take your time."

I headed to the water passing the beach bar and bare breasted European women trying to avoid tan lines. I found a quiet sunny space not too far from the bar but in full view of that beautiful ocean.

Out of the corner of my eye, I noticed a row of Cabana Boys sitting alongside the bar, waiting to see if they can be of any assistance. It was painfully obvious they were just there for the view and not the same view we were there for.

I lay there taking up some sun and was getting a little thirsty. I raised my hand to get one of the Cabana Boys' attention but they acted as if they were all on break or just preoccupied with all the bare tits scattered around. I finally got up and got it. I began to think about Lynn's dare.

I untied my top and pulled it over my head. I threw my extra dark Ann Klein shades on and laid back. It felt strangely liberating and powerful, especially when all of a sudden, I was the most popular hotel guest there.

A nice breeze blew off the water and it was almost chilly making my chocolate nipples stand at attention and sent call men over like a homing signal.

"Can I get you something?"

I opened my eyes to see a tall brown skinned good looking dread head standing in my sun.

"Drink?" He asked again.

"I'll have one, thanks." I accepted.

"Cigarette?"

"Don't smoke!"

"Are you here alone?"

"Nope." I answered with my perfect full breast staring back at him.

"Well, if you need aaany ting, miss lady." His Jamaican accent causing him to drag out the word any.

"Yeah I know, just call."

It was funny that just twenty minutes ago I couldn't get sand kicked on me, now every few seconds my solitude is being disturbed. As I gazed into the water, there seemed to be miles and miles of ocean to get lost in as you relax.

All of a sudden, I felt my sun being blocked again.

"Excuse me baby, do you have a light?"

"Don't smoke," I answered.

"All right thank you, by the way you have a beautiful pair of brown eyes."

"Oh really," I said pulling down my dark shades from my eyes, giving him my 'get the fuck out of here' stare, as he shuffled off to his next bare breasted victim. He gave my beautiful brown eyes a quick once over before he left.

Just as I began to wonder where Lynn was, I felt his hand on mine.

"You did it, you really did it!" He sounded a little surprised that I let them all hang out. He took his rightful place next to me like a King on his throne with drink in hand sipping, laughing and shaking his head.

"Told you I would," I said with a freakish little grin and a raised eyebrow.

"Let me rub some oil on you before you burn."

"Sweetie, I am just too dark to burn."

"You're never too dark to burn, so turn over let me start with your back."

I obediently turned over allowing the sun to bake my buns as Lynn began to pour oil into his hands. He began rubbing them on my butt and then my legs, back to my butt and over my back.

I sipped my drink and enjoyed my lubing. My head was pointed in the direction of the Cabana Boys. I watched them as they envied Lynn, while Lynn was thoroughly enjoying the attention.

After a few minutes, I shut my eyes and took in that soft island breeze. I dreamed of my perfect moment, my perfect vacation, my perfect lover and my perfect life.

I reminisced back to my morning watching a live rendition of deep throat. The look on that man's face as that girl moved up and down hungrily as if that was the best thing she had ever tasted, gave me butterflies.

I wonder where they are now. Is she still on her knees with the wind in her hair, with the sun on her back and a dick in her mouth?

The dream I drifted off into was explicit and raunchy but sexy and inviting staring at my hotel neighbors. He must be really good to her for her to please him so.

We spent the majority of the day toasting our bodies in the Jamaican sun, drinking and holding hands as Lynn kissed my hand periodically.

"Do you want to go sightseeing or shopping?" He asked.

"Now what kind of woman would I be if I turned down shopping? Shopping of course," I declared.

"Well, get your pretty ass up and get dressed."

He won't get an argument out of me. I put on my top, grabbed my skirt, grabbed Lynn's hand and led him back to the room so I could get changed.

"We are painting the town, taking in the sights, and all the tourist attractions."

The Bob Marley Theater was so tourist like and all of the tourist shopping spots were boring to me.

"Lynn baby, can we do some real sightseeing?"

"Sure baby, what do you want to do?"

"I don't know! The tourist attractions are boring as hell."

"Alright, let's do it."

That's what I love about him; he takes charge and always gives me my way. We rode around in a taxi for hours. I had never realized how the currency differs in Jamaica until now.

We just paid four hundred Jamaican dollars for a wrap around skirt and a pocketbook made of coconuts. He took me to the mountains and into town. While there, I realized that these people here are really poor, it's sad.

The Queen should be ashamed of how they did these people. We rode around through the town of Montego Bay as I watched almost in fear for my life. I saw the Jamaican military riding on the back of trucks, automatic weapons in hand. The inner city can really ruin it for you. I guess I should have stuck to the tourist attractions.

AND THEN THERE WERE NONE

Chapter 3

It was almost dinner time and we hadn't figured out what we were going to do. After returning to the hotel, Lynn asked, "Baby, you wanna go out to eat?"

"Sure do!" I answered.

"Let's get a little dressy. I am going to go to the front desk to ask about restaurants in town."

"Babe , you haven't said nothing but a word! I'll jump in the shower and by the time you come back I should be done." I informed him, excitedly.

" Alright, I'll be back in five."

"Take your time," I shouted as I walked toward the bathroom taking off my clothes, tossing them on the bed, as I passed the bedroom.

"Oh, you're just going to walk past me stark naked with that big ass shaking?"

"Yup, sure am." I answered, throwing a little extra swing in my hips and shutting the bathroom door.

"You're wrong Tav, dead wrong," I heard through the bathroom door with a little laugh in his voice. He shouted, "You need to let me put something in that."

I didn't even answer. I pretended not to hear him as I sang over him talking. I don't know what makes him think every conversation about my ass has to end with him putting his dick in it.

As I stood in the bathroom drying and oiling my sun baked body parts with baby oil, Lynn knocked. I barely understood his muffled words as they came through the bathroom door.

"You done?" He shouted.

I cracked the door open and poked my head out with a puff of steam following and answered, "If you just asked whether I was done, the answer is yes. Did you find some place to eat?"

"Yes, I ran into the cab driver in the lobby and he told me about a few places. He gave me his number and said to call when we are ready to go and he would take us."

"Oh good," I answered.

"So hurry up and get dressed!" Lynn demanded.

"I'm coming, I'm coming!" I said, leaving the bathroom to him so that he could freshen up..

"And don't be all day," I said playfully.

"Damn girl, what did you do take a shower in all hot water? It's so steamy in here it looks like the place is on fire."

"Oh shut up and take your shower, silly."

***

Lynn was in and out and I wasn't even dressed yet.

"Damn, you're done?" I said surprisingly when he walked in the room. "I hope you washed that thing good, you never know when I might want to hook you up."

"You wanna come over here and taste it to be sure," he snapped back at me.

"If I do, we will never get out of here."

"Tav, quit playing with me, getting you to give me some head is like pulling teeth." Lynn whined at me.

I kind of brushed it off, stayed silent and finished getting dressed. I actually wanted to hook him up, especially with the new skills I learned from my downstairs neighbor. *I'm not going to say anything, I'll surprise him.*

I put on my sexiest ensemble low cut to the naval with my cleavage in full view; high cut to the hip on both sides with my fuck him girl pumps on. It was giving the illusion that I was six feet tall. I'm only 5'7, but I've got legs for days.

Lynn looked at me seductively and said, "Maybe we should stay in."

"Baby no, I look too good to stay in."

"You'll make a nigga kill somebody dressed like that, damn, you look good."

***

The taxi driver took us on a tour of the nighttime hot spots in Montego Bay. We stopped at a nice little restaurant on the water where we gazed at the incoming cruise ships docking with their cabin lights flickering off the water.

It was a real Kodak moment. Our picture perfect moment was interrupted by the sound of the gentlemen at the next table trying to mimic the accent and the dialect of the islanders when he was speaking to the waiter.

That really irked me when people pulled that mocking crap. Rasta impostors were what I called them.

We had just decided to leave when I noticed exactly who the guy was at the next table fakin' Jamaican. It was my downstairs hotel neighbor and his deep throat companion. I didn't recognize her without his dick in her mouth.

He looked at me as if he recognized me too, he smiled and gave me a thumbs up and said, "Ya Mon, are you two enjoying your vacation?"

"We're having a great time," Lynn responded.

"Have you seen any good sights since you've been here," he asked while rubbing his hand not so discretely from his chest to his crotch.

He was so smooth with his that Lynn hadn't even noticed. A look of embarrassment consumed my face as I broke eye contact with him saying with a stutter, "Yeah, we saw really interesting activities I can't wait to try."

"Yea, like what," he questioned with a slick smile.

"Snorkeling, water skiing and scuba diving. You know those kinds of things."

I quickly changed the subject. After a few awkward moments, we said our good nights and went in opposite directions, continuing our night...

I heard the woman at the table say it was nice to meet you, hope to see you again soon.

We just waved as if to say bye, as I thought you'll be seeing me, sooner than you think. Or, I'll be seeing the back of her head.

We spent the rest of the evening laying on a beach chair at the hotel beach, wrapped in each other's arms. Our legs were intertwined, gently sharing kisses, whispering I love you softly in each other's ears between kisses. We listened to the waves of the ocean crash against the sandy beach, while we heard the sound of calypso music playing in the distance, with sand on our feet and the flicker of tiki torches lighting the walkway.

The moon and stars looked so much closer and clear here, this is truly paradise. How could someone come to this place and not fall in love? I could stay here for the rest of my life living off of love without a care in the world. Just me and my man.

Chapter 4

Today is our last day on the island; it was time to go home. We are leaving in a few hours so we're going to make the best of it. I got up early and did my usual routine. I sat on the balcony in my bathrobe sipping my orange juice and watched the ocean. I could feel the cool breeze from the sea blowing on me, as the palm trees swayed to my same rhythm. I opened my bathrobe exposing my tight chocolate body to the island of Montego Bay allowing the sun to kiss me in the most intimate of places as the wind brushed my braids.

My nipples reacted to the coolness of the wind, lost in thought; the beach became out of focus in my eyes so I shut them and opened my legs. I sat there and ran my hands down between my legs and touched myself again and again. I put my head back and went with it.

I positioned one leg on the banister railing and the other was firmly planted on the floor. I stroked my little man in the boat with my thumb, when I was interrupted by the feel of a third hand helping out. One on my breast and the other worked its way down my pubic area and replaced mine. Lynn positioned his way between my legs on the floor as the wind blew. Lynn blew his warm breath on me.

First, there was one finger, then two fingers in and out over and over licking and sucking until my patio chair was literally on two legs. I could feel his warm saliva mixed with my own juices dripping down to my asshole followed by his tongue. That was new.

Damn, it felt strange so I tried to push his head away but he pulled me closer and licked my asshole again and again. I tried to push him away which made him more determined. I felt the chair come down off of its two legs and meet the other two on the floor. Lynn motioned for me to get up and turn around. He removed my robe and instructed me to lean over the balcony.

There I stood knockers swinging, ass in the air. To anyone downstairs, it would have looked as if I was just admiring the scenery.

Lynn pulled up a chair and placed himself right behind me and buried his head in the crack of my ass. His warm tongue is circling the rim of my poop shoot, every once and awhile allowing it to take a plunge into my asshole. I held on to the rail for dear life breaking one of my acrylic nails in the process.

His fingers fed my wet snatch one after the other. Lynn nibbled and kissed my plump round mounds as he entered my back side with his index finger. I didn't care who was watching, I opened my eyes to look around and there was no one, so I shut my eyes and exhaled. My body was so excited so everything was fair game. Things I said no to in the past were an easy yes right now.

Lynn stood up behind me with his bathrobe open exposing his nude body with his man at attention. He removed his finger from me and replaced it with his man inch by swollen inch into my anal cavity. My knees abandoned me as he stroked faster but gently I wanted to scream, it felt so good, like nothing I've ever felt. My toes curled and it felt as if every hair on my body stood on end.

Waves of orgasms came over me. My mouth filled up with saliva, tears filled up my eyes as his dick filled my back side. There was still a hole unoccupied that was aching for attention, I began to beg in a soft breathy whisper.

I started to say things I wouldn't normally say, "Fuck me" I cried.

"Put your fingers in my pussy, finger fuck my pussy, baby." I pleaded.

I guess my vulgarity excited him even more; he held on to my braids with one hand and worked the hell out of me. With his finger in one hole and his dick in the other, I never knew it to be possible to have an anal orgasm. I was so excited I began to throw it back at him using my hands to help him finger fuck me into a frenzy. I stroked my clitoris until I came; screaming. I felt Lynn's rhythm change to a sporadic off beat stroke as his breathing turned into moans.

He slumped over my back breathing heavy; I could feel the pulsating of his private as he splashed off what felt like gallons into my rear end dripping sweat down my side. I no longer felt the breeze that once blew over my body which now felt like fire to the touch. Out of breath and spasmodic, I fell back onto the chair that once held me on two legs.

I laid my head back and laughed aloud when I noticed the couple in the room above us gazing over there balcony in complete awe. They were staring in amazement so hard and when they noticed me notice them, they couldn't move. I jumped up.

"Oh my God," I screamed as I grabbed my robe and dove for cover inside the room.

"What is it?" Lynn asked, while looking around but still standing on the balcony.

"Look up, someone is watching." I informed him.

Lynn jumped over the threshold; dick still wet and swinging, laughing.

"Damn 'Tavia, you could have told me, you just ran and left a brother."

"Sorry Daddy," I said with a giggle. "I wonder how long they were watching."

"Don't know but they had a bird's eye view!" He said as he lay next to me on the floor.

He began to brush the braids out of my eyes. In his hand were several braids from my head. "Oh shit 'Tavia, your braids are coming out."

I snatched them from his hands inspecting each one carefully for cuticles, totally forgetting about the voyeurs that watched our most intimate moment.

Hell, my vanity kicked in and took over when I thought this man had snatched me bald. I inspected every braid and felt around my head for bald spots, there were none. They just slid off my hair; almost a week of salt water swimming must have weighed heavy on my braids until they began to fall out. However, Lynn's tugging on them didn't help either.

Tired and spent, asshole feeling wiggly and wet; we laid there on the floor staring at the ceiling until we dozed off to sleep. The telephone rang and startled us; waking us from a sound sleep.

"It's noon Mr. Rose," the voice on the other end of the line said. "You asked us to give you a courtesy call to let you know when the shuttle bus was on its way to take you to the airport. It will be here in one hour. Someone will be up soon to pick up your luggage."

"Thank you," Lynn replied and hung up.

"Come on sweetie!" He nudged me. "It's time to get cracking, that was the front desk we've got about an hour."

I jumped up and headed for the shower where Lynn joined me. We were dressed and waiting in the lobby forty five minutes later in silence.

I don't believe we spoke two words to one another all the way to the airport.

***

I sat on the plane twirling my wedding ring back and forth on my finger nervously. I was saddened by the thought of going home because everything here was so perfect. Neither one of us was prepared for it to end.

We sat for about an hour still quiet. I was resting my head on his shoulder and we were holding hands.

"I love you," I said, rubbing his jaw with the back side of my hand.

"I know," he whispered while kissing me with soft pecks on my lips.

Tears began to well up in my eyes and run down my face; one after the other following the same path.

Lynn sat back in his seat to get a good look at me. He grabbed my face with both hands, leaned forward and started kissing my tear drenched cheeks; telling me he loved me after every kiss. My cry sounded as if I was in pain. Lynn pulled me close in his arms to comfort me.

My cries drew the attention of the ladies in the seats two rows ahead of us, who looked on saying aloud, "That's beautiful how much in love they look," as they glared at my wedding ring which left a very noticeable tan mark on my finger.

I removed myself from the seat and began to walk to the lavatory to collect myself when I heard the flight attendant say to Lynn, "Go with her honey, and make sure she's okay."

Lynn grabbed my hand and walked into the tight bathroom with me. I sat on the toilet seat as Lynn kneeled in front of me assuring me every moment we spend together will be just like this past week. He promised. I sat there for a few seconds staring into his eyes.

We both stood up to leave. He kissed my forehead, the tip of my nose and then my lips. I dropped back to the toilet seat, unzipped his zipper and just like that we became members of the mile high club. Closing my eyes, I pulled him out of his pants and placed him in my mouth. I did my best impression of my downstairs deep throating hotel neighbor, not letting up until I felt him grab for things. He couldn't catch hold of his toes.

When his heels touched the floor again, I had a mouth full of his excitement, giving a whole new meaning to the friendly skies. I gave him the professional of a lifetime; I looked up at him thinking to myself where I was going to spit this. He rubbed my head so lovingly, helped me up, pecked me on my lips and for the first time ever I swallowed.

Lynn zipped up his fly after putting his member back in place, backed out of the bathroom and waited at our seats for me. I washed my face and hands and walked back to my seat when one of the women that were sitting a few seats ahead asked me if I was okay. I shook my head yes in reply to her question. I sat down and laid in Lynn's arms the remainder of the trip.

Reassurance in the friendly skies had me believing that nothing between us was going to change when we reached home. We would always keep each other this happy. Our flight touched ground around 10 pm; we exited the plane to the sound of the pilots' voice thanking us for flying American Airlines, and informing us the weather here was 26 degrees and cold.

We walked hand in hand with our fingers intertwined. We were holding on for dear life and we walked a slow stroll like we were taking a walk to death row. Still no words were spoken as we walked from the arrival gate to customs. As we neared the luggage area, we let go of each other's hands and just like that I lost sight of him in the endless sea of on lookers and went right into the waiting arms of my husband.

The unhappiness I felt on the flight home had to be masked with a fake smile as I kissed him hello. He hugged me so tight I nearly lost my breath. There I was wrapped in Calvin's arms after almost a week apart but still searching for Lynn in the crowd.

Although there was no sign of Lynn, I did notice the two women from the rows ahead of us on the plane staring and whispering. At any point, these two strangers could have ended my marriage with one word, deep down I wished they would have so I could stop this charade and move on with my life. I needed them to do for me what I didn't have the courage to do myself.

I love my husband for who he is but I wasn't in love with him anymore. I've just been going through the motions. I must admit I haven't tried to make it work.

The mere thought of him touching me turns my stomach. I feel as if I'm cheating on Lynn.

We took the Whitestone Bridge home and just as we reached the toll, I felt a slight gush coming from my bum; a reminder of the major back door action on the island a few hours ago.

My back rim felt strangely loose but not sore. Lynn was right, if you're turned on enough your body would accommodate almost anything in any orifice. After all that rubbing, licking and petting, I became so well lubricated. He eliminated the ouch factor, and my butt thanked him. There was quite a bit of traffic leaving the Whitestone Bridge to I-95 North, and it was cold. A far cry from the 100 degree paradise I had just left. As our car reached Exit 16, my cell vibrated on my hip.

"Hello," I answered.

My ears were met by my twin sister's voice on the other line, "Hey Stella, you gotcha groove back?"

"Never lost it," I said with giggle. "How'd you know I was home?"

"I called Calvin and asked him what time your flight was coming in."

"Who is that?" Calvin whispered.

"Yvette," I answered.

"Tell nosey ass to mind his business!"

"Okay girl, I'll talk with you tomorrow, we're pulling up in the parking lot."

"Make sure you do, I want details, bitch."

"You're the nosey one," I said laughing. "Good night, Yvette."

"Oh, one more thing."

"What, woman?"

"Did you bring me back something?"

"GOOD NIGHT, YVETTE."

"Night." Her sister laughed.

Calvin was acting really touchy feely and I knew where this was going. I was trying to throw minor hints like feeling jet lagged and a headache was coming on.

"How about I run to the store and get you some Tylenol?"

"Yes, you do that!"

He hastily went to the store and I figured I could be sleep before he came back or fake it, at least. I heard his key in the door so I played like I was asleep. It was not like that mattered because he nestled up next to me, pulling my panties down from behind parking his already erect member right in the crack of my ass.

I tried to play asleep as long as I could but the only way I could still be sleep and not feel him entering me from behind would be if I were in a coma. My excuse for lack of interest was "Honey, I'm exhausted." That didn't stop him.

"All you have to do is lay there," he said.

"Oh, you're so wet! You missed me, huh?"

I didn't answer I just laid there like a bump until Calvin pulled my legs over my head and rammed himself right up my ass.

"Whoa, what are you doing?"

"I know you wanted to try this, so I'm giving you what you want."

No foreplay, no touching, no lube just straight in, the only lubrication was left over from Lynn . I asked him to stop. He was hurting me, but in his mind that meant harder, he was nowhere near as big as Lynn in length or girth but this hurt. It felt like he ripped me a new one and he was showing me no mercy. He pulled himself out of me and shot his load on my stomach, five minutes and he was done from start to finish and snoring. I sat up in the bed and looked over at him in disgust and got up to go to the bathroom. As I wiped myself I saw blood, and a lot of it. I washed up and patted my sore ass dry and went to bed mad thinking about what Lynn might be doing right now.

Welcome home to me.

Chapter 5

Lynn and I continued to rendezvous several times a week, dinner at Yvonne's Southern Cuisine in Pelham, and plenty of short stays on both sides of the Whitestone Bridge. I can never get enough of him. Calvin works at night so it's easy for me to slip away unnoticed and I'm always home before he gets in.

I always forward my home calls to my cell phone in case he called home. Lynn brought me this cell phone so he can keep in contact with me during the times Calvin would be home and, yes, he paid the bill.

I've actually known Lynn longer than Calvin and it used to be just sex, then it graduated to something deeper. When I met my husband, I stopped seeing Lynn. I thought I had found Mr. Right and those days of Mr. Right Now were over.

Five years into my fairytale marriage, the spark went out and it seemed as if I was living with a roommate. That song, "A Stranger In My House" by Tamia became my most requested song. I was living it. I realized the stranger was me, I needed more. We were stagnant.

I wanted children desperately and we had problems conceiving. I went so far as to taking fertility pills and each time I conceived, I'd miscarry. Five miscarriages later, my body was spent and emotionally I was a mess. Calvin never understood having a child was what I needed most in this world. He wanted one also; however, he could have lived without it at this point.

I was done trying, it just wasn't meant to be. Calvin began to throw himself into his work and so did I, working different shifts and about 50 hours a week. I was lonely.

Lynn had always stayed on my mind so I picked up the phone and began to dial 1-516 -9 and hung up midway through dialing and asked myself, *what are you thinking?*

Lynn is not going to want to talk to me especially after the way I broke it off was so wrong. I figured what the hell? The worst he could do was hang up. So I began to dial again and on the second ring, he answered.

"Hello, 'Tavia, he said into my ear.

"Hi sweetie, how did you know it was me?"

"Tav, I have always kept your number programmed in my phone."

"I miss you," I whispered and just like that we were back on. No questions asked.

We picked up where we left off but with a little extra baggage, my husband.

I knew Lynn was seeing someone, but for us it has always been this way through every relationship he had. I was always the other woman. Those relationships meant nothing which is why I was always there.

When Lynn and I get together sometime we'd have a few drinks but this night we were throwing them back like sailors. We were visiting at his boy Ron's house when Lynn got a phone call. The voice on the other end of the phone told him his grandfather died.

Lynn was hurt. He was devastated. He and his grandfather were very close. This was the first time I had ever seen him cry. We were drinking so much it was clear Lynn was too drunk to drive himself home so he was going to stay at Ron's. It was getting late and it was time for me to go over the bridge back to New Rochelle. Lynn fell into a deep drunken slumber.

"Lynn, I'm leaving," I explained, shaking him to wake him up. It was getting late.

Looking up at me from his depressed drunken state he pleaded with me, "Tavia, please don't leave me tonight. Stay with me!"

"Lynn I can't, it's already two in the morning. You know I have to beat Calvin home."

He buried his head deep in my cleavage with his hands tightly around my waist, "Please Tav, I need you tonight."

How do you say no to that? I kicked my shoes off and curled up next to him on Ron's pull out sofa, my man needed me. How could I deny him?

Just then, my cell phone rang, it was Calvin. I put my finger to Lynn's lips to silence him and answered trying to sound sleep.

"Hello," I said with a whisper.

"Hey, whatcha doin?"

"Babe, I fell asleep reading."

"I was just calling to check on you."

"I'm okay but I'm tired I'll see you in the morning when you come home." We both said goodnight and hung up.

Lynn never looked up. He just kissed the finger I laid softly on his lips. He was hurting, I had to comfort him anyway I could. I helped him get undressed and I climbed on top of him but he pushed me off. He just wanted to be with me, he didn't want to make love.

I wanted him even more. I wanted to console my grieving man so I took him gently in my mouth until I knew some of his tension was gone. I snuggled up next to him and shut my eyes. Lynn held me and I rubbed his head until he was asleep. I figured I would wait until he fell asleep and I could sneak out but the next time I opened my eyes it was daybreak.

The sound of my cell phone ringing woke me. It was Calvin. I wouldn't dare answer it, not until I could think of a good lie and get my alibi straight. While I was reaching for my clothes, I noticed the time.

"Oh shit," I said out loud. "It's 8:45 AM! I'm late, Lynn. I have to go."

He jumped up. "What time is it?" he asked.

"It's 8:46."

"I'm late for work."

"Yes you are. I'm late, I've got to go." I said.

I kissed Lynn goodbye, jumped in my truck and dialed my sister.

When she answered, I asked had Calvin called her.

"As a matter of fact, he did."

"Oh God 'Vette, what did he say?"

"Well lucky for you sister dear, he called when I was in the shower and I missed his call. I was just checking my messages when you called me. I haven't had a chance to call him back yet, I take it your daredevil ass ain't home?" She asked.

"No, I stayed the night with Lynn." I admitted.

The whole fucking night, Octavia, are you crazy?"

"Not now, 'Vette, I know I fucked up. And I have to think of a lie quick."

"Octavia, I know you don't want to hear this but you're gonna fuck around and end up by your damn self."

"You're right! I don't want to hear it, Yvette. Mind your business, let me handle this."

"All right, that must be your final answer. You are the weakest link, twin, goodbye."

She hung up on me. My cell phone rang again. Again, it was Calvin. My stomach was beginning to hurt. What the hell would I say? The phone rang four more times and stopped. My hands were shaking because I was so nervous. I called my sister back, the phone rang five times. No this bitch ain't making me sweat! She answered in her sweetest greeting, pretending like she didn't know who it was.

"Chello."

"Yvette stop playing, I need your help!"

"No, you said you can handle this by yourself, well handle it then."

"I need your help right now; can you bitch at me later?"

"What do you need, Tavia," she blurted, sounding annoyed.

I could picture her rolling her eyes with the slow head turn. She's good for that shit.

I guess when it comes to the nice and evil twin thing you can guess who the evil one is.

"I need you to avoid Calvin's calls today, I'm going to tell him you called me because you lost your keys, were locked out of our car and needed me to bring you the spare in Brooklyn."

"Brooklyn? I don't know a damn soul in Brooklyn."

"Alright I'll say Queens then, do you know anybody in Queens?"

"Ok! What else?" And what time was this?"

"Let's say 6 AM, alright Poncho?"

"Is that it?"

"Yeah, I'll call you later." I informed her.

"Whatever, nigga!"

She hung up. I know she was a bit pissed off, but she'd get over it.

My cell phone rang again I answered it with a nervous "Hello". It was Calvin.

"What happened? You didn't come home last night!" He shouted in my ear.

"Pump your breaks, baby. Of course I came home last night! Wasn't I there when you called?"

"Yeah, but that was around midnight and the bed hasn't been slept in."

"Well hubby," I said, sounding really sarcastic since I got my lie together. "I fell asleep on the sofa watching television and my sister called me to bring her spare key, she was stranded in Queens. So I jumped up and went to help her out. I still have on my same clothes from yesterday."

"What time was that?"

"Around six and I really don't appreciate the interrogation."

"Oh," he said sounding really apologetic. "I'm sorry but the bed hadn't been slept in and I..."

"And you what? Jumped to conclusions," I said sucking my teeth. "I'll be home in about 10 minutes, would you like me bring you breakfast?"

"Yea baby, please." He answered.

"Okay, see you in a few."

Somehow I managed to fuck up and make him apologize. I hung up feeling rather bad for staying out all night, lying and getting Yvette involved. My phone rang again but this time it was Lynn.

His voice mellow and soothing as usual, he said, "Thank you baby," and somehow all that guilt I felt five minutes ago was gone and nobody else mattered.

Lynn flew to Florida to spend time with his grandmother and attend his grandfather's funeral. I threw myself into my work trying to avoid Calvin. I don't know why I treat him so bad.

I should just tell him I'm in love with someone else and that I wanted a divorce but I'm a coward. Maybe he'll get tired of my shit and leave me and then Lynn and I can be together. Maybe then, I could be guilt free. The trick is to not let him catch me with Lynn and make him think the break up is his fault.

Leave it to me to cheat on a perfectly faithful and decent man but it's just not there. I'm guessing I'll be that woman that makes every woman he deals with after me suspect in his eyes. If I get caught, I'd be turning a good man into a dog. But as long as Lynn was in my life, I didn't care.

Lynn and I had been spending so much time together that I'd been neglecting my friends. So while he's away, I'll get up with my girlfriend Pearl and catch up on some girl time.

I took a ride to Lefrack City, picked her up and did some shopping. We stopped by the liquor store, grabbed a bottle of Amaretto, went back to her place and caught up on old times. Before we knew it, the bottle was empty and we were tipsy laughing and joking at everything until she asked, "So, how's that husband of yours?"

"I don't know, I guess he's fine."

"What do you mean 'you guess he's fine,' you're still together, aren't you?"

"Yeah, but..."

"But what? You know my mother always told us when someone says but, that's when you should listen."

"But I'm not happy anymore and Lynn is back in my life."

"I would say I'm sorry to hear that but I never liked Calvin." My friend admitted.

"Never?" I asked.

He's not good enough for you." She voiced her opinion.

"He's not good enough for me? Well, who is good enough for me? Lynn?" At that moment I realized she never responded when I told her I was back with Lynn. I wanted to see her reaction.

"Me," she said, swapping her lipstick with mine. She grabbed the back of my head with both her hands and kissed me. I yanked back.

"What are you doing?"

"You know what I'm doin', it's me you should be with." She placed another kiss square on my lips. This time she added some tongue.

"Whoa, Whoa, Whoooooa, slow down speedy." Just then, I realized her hand was rubbing the inside of my thigh closer to the crotch of my pants. I politely removed it, feeling embarrassed and not trying to offend her. It was funny how she was violating me and I didn't want to offend her.

She came in close to my ear and whispered, 'Tavia, you ever been with a woman?"

"That would be a no! I think we both have had too much to drink."

"No, I haven't."

 "Well, maybe you need a little more to drink."

"Can you move over? I'm feeling a little claustrophobic."

"Aren't you even curious to know what it would be like?"

"Not really and I think maybe it's time for me to go."

"Don't leave Tav, I'm sorry," she said, moving out of my personal space creating a gap between us on the sofa.

"But think about it, okay. It's incredibly hard for me to exercise self-restraint when I'm around you."

Now the female psyche is a funny thing. Something I never gave any thought to in the past is weighing heavy on my mind. The tension between us was getting thick and she knew what she was doing. She planted the seed now she was going to sit back and watch it grow.

Everyone knows a woman's curiosity is a dangerous thing. We sat there in awkward silence until I felt I was sober enough to drive home. I got up and began gathering my things and walked to the door.

"Where are you going? It's early."

"Girl, I am going home. I've got to work in the morning." Pearl grabbed my hand, reached over and went in for the kiss as if we were on a date. I turned my head and gave her my cheek. She kissed me softly on my jaw and whispered, "I hope I didn't do irreversible damage to our friendship but..."

Oh God, here comes the but, I thought to myself.

"I'll do whatever it takes to have you even if it means having a threesome with you and Lynn. Ask Lynn", she continued. "That's every man's fantasy and you can give that to him with me."

I'm sure the look on my face screamed that she was crazy, but I didn't say a word. As I was walking down the hall to the elevator, I looked back and she was still standing in the doorway as I stepped foot in the elevator.

"Think about it." She yelled down the hall. As the elevator door shut so did her apartment door.

***

That ride over the Throgs Neck Bridge was the longest; I was still a little tipsy. I got lost in thought. I began saying out loud what I should have said to her when I was there.

"Me, you and Lynn, Bitch, please!"

However, the more I said it, the more I thought about it.

"That is every man's fantasy," I echoed.

Pearl's a good looking girl, 5 ft 3 inches and about 130 pounds. She had a big ass and big boobs, small waist and she was high yellow. She has a Coca Cola bottle shape.

I'm sure Lynn wouldn't object, although, they have never seen each other. What am I saying? This is crazy? This damn girl actually has me contemplating this ridiculous foolishness. Our conversation, no matter how obscene, wouldn't let me go. Better yet, I wouldn't let go of it.

***

Lynn called this morning. He said he'd be home in a few days and we made plans to get up on Wednesday. I missed his birthday because he wasn't here.

"What have you been doing since I've been away?"

"Nothing. Working and hanging out with Pearl."

"Pearl? Oh, your girlfriend in Lefrack?"

"Yeah, I haven't seen her in awhile."

"You used to talk about her a lot. When can I meet her?" Lynn asked.

"You want to meet her? For what?"

"Tavia, I want to know everybody you know. Baby, I'm not going anywhere." He assured me.

That sounds so sweet, he deserves a threesome. One time won't hurt. He's the perfect man. I know he'll never leave because he's been here all these years.

All the typical threesome questions went through my mind. Will he like her? Would he creep around with her behind my back? And could I handle seeing him make love to another woman? Then I thought, *what the hell, it would be his birthday present.*

"Tavia, I miss you."

"I miss you too."

"I picked up the phone to call you a few times but I remembered he was home and your cell was off. What's up, you know that's the only way I can get in touch with you."

"Do I detect a hint of jealousy?"

"Hell yeah, you do."

"Are you serious?"

"Yes I am! Are you two working it out 'Tavia? Let me know?"

"Baby if it's reassurance you want, not a problem, you're all I want. I won't even let him touch me. So don't be like that. I'm saving it all for you."

"Baby, it's hard not seeing you when I want to and not having you when I need you. This has got to stop."

"I know honey," I said as tears began welling up in my eyes. "Just give me a little more time."

"Sorry to put this on you 'Tavia, but I want you all to myself."

His voice turned to a whisper and I could barely hear him, "I gotta go."

Before I could say goodbye, he hung up. That was strange. I didn't get an I love you. He must really be hurting and stressing over his grandfather's death.

Just then my cell phone rang and it was Pearl. Before I could say hello she said, "Hi mama, did you think about it?"

"Yeah I did and I have to admit you caught me off guard." A sudden boldness came over me as I informed her.

"This is what we are going to do. Lynn is coming home Wednesday and guess what?" I waited for her to answer.

"What," she inquired.

"You're going to be his present."

Without a hint of hesitation she blurted out, "So what time are you picking me up?"

"Around six o'clock."

"I knew you would come around. I'll see you then."

I surprised myself. I was about to share my man and I love him so much and I didn't even care.

The next few days were like waiting for Christmas. I stopped by the adult toy store and picked up some lube and condoms. Lynn and I never used them. He knows I can't conceive but I don't want to run the risk of him getting her pregnant. I hit the Throgs Neck Bridge to Pearl's house. Lynn and I planned to meet on my side of the bridge at the Capri Motor Inn in the Bronx.

So right before Pearl and I got a short stay, we hit the liquor store. I figured I would need a drink just in case I lost my nerve.

By the time Lynn got there, we already downed a half a pint of E&J and I was feeling bold.

"Go in the bathroom, he's here," I told her.

"What room are you in," Lynn questioned.

"17."

He knocked on the door. I opened the door wearing nothing but a red thong and shoes, and of course my pretty smile. I kissed him on his lips and said, "I missed you."

The scene was perfect. Candles were flickering and the radio was playing our favorite *Chocolate Factory* CD. I poured him a drink and sat him down in the chair near the door. I stood behind him, wrapped my arms around his neck and said "Happy belated birthday."

As I was unbuttoning his shirt, I told him I had something for him. Pearl emerged from the bathroom wearing the almost identical ensemble as I was. Lynn jumped damn near out the chair.

"What's going on, Tavia," he demanded.

"Relax sugar, this is your Birthday present."

"Tav, I don't have any condoms."

"I got you," I answered back while pointing to the Trojans on the nightstand.

He looked over at the bottle of E&J and stated, "You two have been in here drinking, are you sure?"

"I'm positive, it's okay." And to my surprise, I was really okay with it.

"You just sit there for a minute and enjoy the show."

I walked over to the bed where Pearl was sitting, sat next to her and touched her gently on her bare breast first with my hand then with my mouth. I used my hand to motion her to lie down and I kissed her cheek, rubbing my body against hers. I patted her on the hip telling her to open her legs as I slid my well-manicured nails down her body and latched on to her thong, pulling them down and then off. I looked over at Lynn to see if he was enjoying the show. He sat there expressionless sipping his drink.

I then crept down between her thighs and licked her, kissed her and sucked her most private parts. Pearl pulled me up by my hair and kissed me on my neck rolling over on top, returning the favor. We made love to each other like a well-choreographed dance.

Lynn still sat there, where I put him, noticeably aroused by the sight of us. I pulled Pearl off the bed by her hand and placed her on her knees between Lynn's open legs. I stood behind him and instructed her to suck him.

As his zipper went down, he began to kiss me. The look on Pearl's face was shock at the size of what popped out. The moment was so heated that the window in the room was beginning to fog. I opened the Trojan paper with my teeth, handed it to Lynn and with one hand he unrolled the condom over his massive member.

Somehow, the three of us ended up on the bed taking turns with my man. We laid there panting and sweaty in the mess we made. Lynn kissed me, reached over me and kissed her and instantly my blood began to boil. I didn't mind sharing his dick, but his kiss is sacred to me. Kissing is personal and he knows that. It took me a long time to kiss him but I didn't say a word.

Lynn looked at his watch, jumped up and got in the shower. I followed, figuring I can get some 'in the shower lovin,' he held my face and said, "I didn't cum with her."

"I don't care about that but you kissed her." I said.

"You didn't say that kissing wasn't allowed."

"I didn't think I had to."

"I'm sorry."

I began soaping myself up and changed the subject.

"Why are you leaving so soon? Are you angry with me?" I asked.

"Are you kidding? Angry no, you just fulfilled every man's fantasy. That was something I always said I wanted to do before I got married."

Married? I thought he was making plans to ask me to marry him. He was just waiting for me to divorce Calvin. I didn't want to get too excited.

I didn't even change my facial expression. I continued to rinse off and stepped out of the shower, wrapping my towel around me.

"I've got something I have to take care of but I'll make it up to you," he said, stepping out behind me.

I figured he had to tell somebody so he was leaving to brag to Ron.

Pearl was still laying there as naked as the day she was born. She was smoking a tightly rolled blunt. She waved goodbye to Lynn as he passed as he made his way to the door.

Lynn turned to wave goodbye to Pearl, kissed me and sucked my bottom lip into his mouth.

"What's her name," he asked.

I had gotten so caught up in the moment that I forgot to introduce them properly.

"Do you really care?"

"No, not really," he confessed laughing as he walked out the door. "I only have eyes for you 'Tavia."

I turned to Pearl and exhaled. I sat on the end of the bed with my back to her.

"I guess it's time to go."

"Not so fast, I only did him for you. Now, what you gonna do for me?"

Damn it, there's always a catch.

"You just had me!" I exclaimed.

"Not the way I wanted you. If sharing you with him was the way I had to have you then it was no problem. However, girlfriend, he's gone now and it's just us." Pearl said.

I reached for my drink and turned it up. I stood up and dropped my towel to the floor.

"Let's do the damn thing."

Chapter 6

The one night out of the week that Calvin is off we spent it living in different parts of the apartment until bedtime. If he's in the bedroom, I'm in the living room. There used to be a time when whichever part of the house he was in, I was in.

Now I'd do anything to avoid sex with him all together, it didn't matter what day it was. I was feeling sick and sluggish; I think I was coming down with the flu or something. I can't hold anything down. I can barely lift my head from this pillow so it's best I stay away from Calvin so I don't give him whatever I have.

I felt like I was cut off from Lynn when Calvin was home. I was going to sneak a call in but just when I went to dial my house phone, my cell phone rang.

"Hello," I answered.

"Hey lady, how are you feeling?" Lynn asked.

"I feel miserable."

"Poor baby, need your man to come take care of you?"

"I wish you could," I admitted.

Calvin walked in the room so I tried to be discreet and became very evasive.

Lynn could tell by my tone that Calvin was there so he began to fuck with me.

"I miss you," he said.

"Uh huh."

"I love you."

"I know," I giggled, laughing like I just heard the funniest joke.

"Can you sneak out?"

"No girl, you are so crazy," I answered.

"No! That's a first, you sure? I'll make you feel better."

Why do men think dick is the answer to everything?

"Um, I'll see."

"I wanna see how much you love me." Lynn said.

"Didn't I do that already?"

"I'm up the block from your house at the Carib."

"What! What the hell are you doing up there?"

Calvin looked at me. I pointed to the phone and whispered, "It's my crazy sister, and she's in Philly. Crazy girl drove all the way there for a Cheesesteak."

"Your sister is a nut, glad I married the tamed twin," he replied and walked into the kitchen.

Tamed twin, I thought. My sister doesn't do half the dumb shit I do or that I lead him to believe she does. Hell, if he only knew, he *did* marry the wild sister.

I turned my attention back to Lynn on the phone and whispered, "Give me thirty minutes then meet me in front of KFC."

"Don't disappoint me, 'Tav!"

I hung up the phone and pretended to be even sicker than I was.

"Calvin," I summoned.

"Yeah, 'Tav."

"My neck is hurting; it's starting to get stiff."

"You want me to rub it for you?"

"That will make it worse." He always uses massages as an excuse to get some. For some reason, that was foreplay for him. "I need a heating pad and your sister has mine."

"No she doesn't, she left it at my mom's house."

"Would it be too much trouble to ask you to go get it for me?"

"You want me drive all the way to the Bronx this time of night?"

"It's only eleven o'clock."

"Alright, I'll go."

That was almost too easy. No argument or fuss. I wasn't going to sweat it.

That gave me at least an hour and a half because he can never go to his mom's and come right back. As soon as I saw his car pull off, I jumped up, hopped in the shower and threw on my Victoria secret T-shirt dress.

I was about to get my period, so to be on the safe side I put this new rubber like cup inside to catch any blood that may come down. It's neater than tampons and you can have sex with it in. This took all of 10 minutes and before I knew it I was heading up the block to KFC. Lynn sat looking pleased with himself because he knew he had me wrapped around his finger.

I parked my ass in the car and told him to drive to the high school and pull around the back to the parking lot. We hopped in the back seat of his Navigator and his little man was already at attention. He reached his hands under my T-shirt and realized I was going commando.

"No panties, huh?"

"Easy access."

I climbed on top of him, put my hips to work and forgot all about being sick. Maybe he did have a point. Sex was the answer.

By the time Lynn was finished with me, I had sweat out my perm and probably my flu too.

"Take me home, I have to get back before Calvin."

"Let's chill for a minute," he giggled because he knew I couldn't.

He drove me home and as I was getting out of the truck, I kissed him goodnight and he grabbed my hand.

"I'm getting tired of sharing you, Tav." Lynn admitted.

That threw me off. I always thought he was fine with the arrangement.

"Me too," I replied as I reached over and pecked him on his cheek.

I jumped out the truck burdened with his last words as I waved him goodbye.

As soon as I walked inside the door, I locked it. I heard Calvin coming towards the door because for some reason his keys make a distinct jingle. I damn near leaped over the sofa to get back in my sick bed I had made up on the chaise. Calvin came and sat near me rubbing some oil his mother sent for my neck on my skin.

"Your skin feels clammy," he blurted. "You must have on too many covers."

"No, I'm trying to sweat this cold out."

Damn, I just remembered the *Instead* I placed inside me before I ran out. I got up went to the bathroom, and put my finger as far inside of me as I could to pull it out but I couldn't reach it.

I sat on the toilet and tried again but it was too far out of reach. *Oh God, Lynn got this damn thing lodged inside me.* I went in my room got the box the *Instead* came in. I got my cell phone and dialed the 24 hour 1-800 number and shut myself up in the bathroom. A woman answered after a while.

"Hello and thank you for calling *Instead*, how can I help you?"

"I used your *Instead* and had sex, now this damn thing is stuck in me."

"Well, Miss, don't panic," the voice on the other end of the phone said.

It was too late; my panic was in warp speed right now. Don't panic? She's not the one with a giant rubber thing stuck in her.

"Look, I can't get it out! I've tried every position on the instructions for removal."

"Who are you talking to in there?" I heard Calvin's voice from outside the bathroom door.

"I'm on the phone with Yvette again." I yelled out.

"Tell her to bring me a cheesesteak."

Damn! What the hell is he doing listening outside the bathroom door? I turned the sink on to muffle the sound of me talking in the bathroom and stood in the shower as far away from the bathroom door as possible.

"Hello, are you still there," the woman questioned.

"Yes I'm sorry, go ahead."

"Alright, I need you to calm down first, put your back against the wall and squat down with your knees apart. Insert your finger into the vagina and hook your finger under the rim and pull."

"I can't reach it."

"Okay, try it again, now bear down."

I bored down with everything I had and the only thing that came out was Lynn's deposit and a fart.

"Try that same position but sit on your toilet."

"Look I am digging as far as I can, and I can't reach it."

"Well, miss," the voice said. "Keep trying or go to the emergency room."

"Is that it? Is that all you can do for me?"

"I'm sorry miss; we never had a problem like this before, but thank you for using *Instead*. Good night."

No this bitch didn't hang up on me! Hell, I can't go to the Emergency Room tonight! What the hell would I tell Calvin? I know he'd want to come with me.

Shit! Shit! Shit! I guess I'm going to have to go to the Doctor tomorrow to get this thing out of me.

I took my T-shirt off and turned the shower on. I stood there with the hot water spraying in my face asking myself. "How do you get yourself in such a mess all the time?"

Well, I didn't have an answer for myself. I just got out the shower and got in the bed.

***

I got up early, not to primp and look pretty like I do for Lynn, but to figure out how to get away from Calvin today. So I got on the horn and called Yvette.

"What you doing today," I asked.

"It's Saturday, going to get my nails done."

"Good I'm coming with you, and by the way you were in Philly last night." I told her.

"For what?"

"For a cheesesteak."

"What kind of shit did you put me in now, Pinocchio?"

"I'll tell you later, and I'll call you back after I call Stephen."

My Doctor and I have a very informal doctor patient relationship. He calls me 'Tavia and I call him Stephen, it's kinda strange. It used to be uncomfortable calling my GYN by his first name but he insisted. He's been my doctor for about ten years. So I guess if I am comfortable enough to have him between my legs, then calling him Stephen should be easy.

I hung up and called my Doctor to see if he'd see me today.

"What's the problem, 'Tavia?"

"I have this *Instead* Tampon stuck inside of me and I can't get it out."

"Okay, I'll squeeze you in around noon. How's that?"

"That works. Thank you, see you then."

I picked up my evil twin, filling her in on my dilemma and letting her know what role she played in my saga today.

"That's what your ass gets. Sick as hell but you still run out in the street to see this dude. Maybe that thing being stuck up your ass is a wakeup call." My sister said.

"Can we not have this conversation, 'Vette. Please?"

"Still don't want to hear about your bull, 'Tavia. You're not going to be happy until you find yourself by yourself, but I am going to tell you anyway. Calvin is a good man and you're married to him, you might want to make it work. What do you and Lynn have?"

I couldn't answer because the nausea was churning my stomach and the more I spoke the more I felt like throwing up. I shut up and took my tongue lashing like a woman.

"Octavia you're going to mess around and get caught, I can't half keep up with your lies. But if you don't leave Lynn alone, leave Calvin alone. Hell bitch, make a damn choice! You can't keep having your cake and eat it too. You're gonna be the one hurting in the end." My sister schooled me.

Everything after that I tuned out but she was right and it brought me back to Lynn's last words to me the night before about being tired of this arrangement.

I couldn't bring myself to hurt Calvin but what she had to realize was the difference for Lynn was that he had my heart...

I wanted to tell her so bad about the threesome Lynn and I had. I know she'd bust my bubble and call me stupid for doing that so I kept it to myself.

***

I went into Stephen's office and he informed me I was due for my yearly annual, but first we'd deal with the problem at hand. I got undressed completely, put on the gown open to the front, put my feet in those stirrups and scooted down to the end of the table. Stephen knelt between my parted legs and turned on that hot ass light. Then I felt the urge to fart. Every time I feel that heat from that lamp, I get the uncontrollable urge to break wind.

"Tavia, the next time you want to try a new feminine product, ask me about it first," he said as he was pulling the foreign object out of me.

"You don't have to worry," I answered. "I threw those damn things away."

He completed his exam and asked me to pee in a cup. I went to the bathroom handled my business, put the cup through the hole in the wall and went back to the exam room to get dressed. Just as I was leaving Stephen sat down in his office and said that we needed to talk. He looked so serious. I sat down quick. In the past I've had abnormal paps, so I began to think the worst.

"What's the problem?"

"You're pregnant." The doctor informed me.

"I'm what, that's not possible."

"Oh it's very possible, when was your last period?"

I thought about it for a minute. It has been awhile. I have been having such a good time with Lynn I totally forgot I didn't get it and now it's June.

"March," I answered. "That explains why I have been feeling so sick. I thought I had the flu," I added.

"And you didn't get worried when your period didn't show?"

I just shook my head no.

"I'm going to need you to make an appointment for an ultrasound, so we can see how far along you are."

"I don't believe this, how did this happen?" I asked, really sounding puzzled.

How'd this happen? You know how it happened. I thought you'd be happy. I know you and Calvin have been trying for a long time."

I mean I know how it happened, but what he didn't know was I stopped trying. I gave up on trying to have a baby with Calvin. And hell, this baby wasn't his.

I couldn't even finish my sentence. I just walked out of the office and headed to the car where my sister sat waiting, yapping on her cell phone. I had to put on a normal look because I wasn't ready to tell her yet. Hell, I don't know if I should feel happy or upset.

What is Lynn going to say? How do I tell him? How do I tell Calvin? Maybe I just won't tell him. This will give me the courage to leave Calvin and Lynn and I can be together.

I could feel butterflies dancing in my gut or was it the nausea playing tag in my insides. I'm in total disbelief and my day was ruined. How could I be so careless? I badgered myself over and over again.

"Which nail place do you want to go to, Yvette?"

"My salon is closed today so let's go to Ghetto Headquarters."

Of course it's not the real name but it's around the corner from the Projects on one of the busiest streets in New Rochelle and today it was crowded as hell.

We were going to be here all day; everybody from the hood gets their nails done there. This place is where the most catfights and arguments break out and all the good gossip is spread. I hate this place but if you ever want to know who's fucking whose man or who's the latest HIV victim, who's getting high or just what went on in Toby's, which was a popular hood bar across the street, Ghetto Headquarters was your place.

And just as I suspected, we walked in on an argument. One girl, way in the back drying her nails, was arguing with another girl in the front, getting her nails polished, about her HIV status.

"You know you got that shit, bitch," the girl in the back yelled.

"No I don't, I'll show you my papers," the girl in the front replied.

"Bitch please! I heard your man was on the list."

"He was not!" She yelled, as she defended her man's masculinity. "Did you see the list? Well then, mind your business."

Yvette and I sat in the chairs in between them waiting for our turn, moving our head from side to side like we were watching a tennis match.

Yvette turned to me and said out loud, "A list?"

Apparently there was a death list left behind of all the guys in this town that slept with this guy who died from complications due to A.I.D.S

"Yeah and that bitch's man is on it," a voice yelled from the back of the nail salon.

"Say word," Yvette said laughing, hysterically. "A bunch of guys on the DL playing tough guy, but sliding up into another guy is just downright nasty.

Yvette spoke loudly because she didn't care who heard her.

"Wait a minute! Wait a damn minute! Who left the list?" Yvette was laughing so hard that her laughs turned to snorts.

"The dead guy." I answered.

"The dead guy left a list?"

"Yeeeess,'Vette, before he died he supposedly left a list of all the so called straight guys that were dissing him in public but digging him out on the low."

"Oh my God," Yvette cried, laughing so hard she nearly fell out the chair.

"Yvette shhhh," I whispered.

"I don't give a flying fuck if they didn't want people in their business they wouldn't be talking about it here."

"Vette stop it," I mumbled.

"Why? She can't beat me, she needs to stop giving me the dirty looks and take that shit up with her man."

"You're embarrassing me, stop playing devil's advocate," I mumbled through clinched teeth.

"You're embarrassed? How you think home girl feel's with her man fucking other dudes on the L? You can't buy this kind of comedy," she blurted, still laughing and snorting. "Stop it, stop it," she bawled. Gasping for air, she said, "I'm gonna pee on myself."

"I don't make this shit up, I just report it," the voice from the back yelled out.

I heard a chair screech and the nail polish began to fly, the girl in the front pushed her chair back with her foot and threw a bottle of nail polish and hit the girl under the nail dryer right in the forehead. They went at each other like two wild cats.

Weaves were being snatched out, freshly done silk wraps were popping off, wet finger and toenails were smudged. Little Asian ladies were huddled in a corner screaming, "You go now, you go now, leave." The Asian man was on the phone with no doubt New Rochelle's Finest.

I turned to 'Vette, "Look what the hell you started," I said, trying not to laugh. Just then the police came in and removed both girls in handcuffs and wet nails. Half of the people waiting were outside being nosey. The police were there in no time. They must have the New Rochelle PD on speed dial because some shit is always jumping off.

As the two girls were being dragged out into the waiting squad car, you could hear one of the girls yelling, "Can I dry my nails first officer,"

She was so serious that even the cop had to laugh.

The little Asian lady yelled, "Next!"

'Vette got up to take her seat and said, "I didn't start it, but think of it this way we will be out of here sooner than we expected."

It's never a dull moment in this place but right now I had my own bullshit to tend with. Next month the topic of conversation up in here might be me.

I just wanted to get my nails done and be gone. My sister loves this gossip shit, as long as it is not about her. I have always been a very secretive, private, non-confrontational type of person. I'm the quiet sneaky mild mannered twin. Yvette was the more straight forward and honest type with a temper, whose reputation for kicking an ass or two preceded her. When she began to egg the argument on, that girl didn't want any of her. She ran straight for the girl in the back.

As we were leaving, Yvette admitted, "I don't care what you say Tavia. I love this place, all the good gossip goes down in here and I thought Wendy had the heat. This place is *fire*." She yelled out loud, mimicking the sound effects on the Wendy Williams radio show, "How you doin'..."

Chapter 7

Yvette and I pulled up in front of the church at the same moment my cell phone started ringing. I looked at it and my heart skipped a beat, it was Lynn. It's not like he knew that I was pregnant but I'm afraid I may tell on myself. The phone rang once more I answered in my sweetest voice possible, "Hello."

"Hello, love of my life. Hey Mama, what are you doing today?"

"I'm going to church."

"Church?" He laughed. "Why? Did someone die?" He joked.

"No, no one died smart ass. Yvette and I just decided we needed some Jesus in our lives today."

"Your sister is with you? Oh hell, tell everyone in the church to get out. The church is going to burst into flames and burn down. The Devil twins are in the building."

"Devil twins?"

"Yes, Devil twins! I wonder if God knew what he was doing making two of you."

"He was thinking he did such a good job making one, he'll make two and then break the mold."

I turned to Yvette. "Yvette, Lynn said the church was going to burst into flames and burn to the ground cause we're here."

"Tell Lynn I said fuck him."

"I heard that," he laughed on the other end of the phone. "That's your sister's job." He continued.

"Yes it is," I interjected.

Lynn and Yvette have a love hate relationship. He loves to fuck with her and she loves to curse him out. He hates her candidness and she hates the fact that he has a girl. But they do have one thing in common and that was that they both loved me.

"Seriously 'Tav, what are you doing later?" Lynn asked.

"Calvin and I are having dinner with his mother."

"Oh, alright," he whimpered, sounding a little disappointed. "Call me later if you can. Ok?"

"Sure baby, bye bye."

Lynn never says goodbye when he hangs up and that kind of irks me. He's really the last person I need to talk to before church especially in my current state of mind.

I need to be in church; maybe I can get some clarity. I haven't been to church since our grandmother passed away. I just couldn't find my way here. It's not the same without her sitting in the front of the church with her big white hat on with the rest of the church mothers, constantly looking back to make sure her family was there.

It's been that way since we were kids. We grew up in the church and it was funny the only time I come to church now is when I have a problem. I was a pure demon for the past two years and now I need Jesus. It was a good thing God was a forgiving God.

While sitting in church looking for answers to my secret problem, it seemed as if Pastor Clark was in my head. He based his sermon on adultery, fornication, and lies and the fact that God sees all. He made sure to let us know that what's done in the dark always comes to light.

Damn, who told him? Is God sending me a personal sermon?

I've cheated on my husband and I had the proof of my infidelity growing inside of me. Now that I think about it Lynn just might be right, the church just might burst into flames just from my presence alone. I'm going to Hell.

As I sat there waddling in my own little sea of deceit, Yvette frantically patted my leg and pointed across the church. I thought for a minute Jesus appeared to escort my sinning ass directly to Hell in a brimstone laced chariot.

"What," I whispered.

"Look," she said whispering back. "Right there! Look in the eighth pew from the front, in the brown suit and yellow shirt."

"Shhhhhhhhhhhhhh!" Sister Johnson scolded us like she did when we were ten. She turned all the way around with her big yellow hat with a feather in it and she rolled her big eyes with her inch long fake lashes at us, then turned back around and faced Pastor Clark.

We both bulged our eyes and smirked at the back of her big bird hat shaking our heads, mimicking her the same way we did when we were younger.

Yvette put one finger up in a wait one minute position, reached in her *Fendi* bag and pulled out a pen and sticky note pad just like she did when we were ten and began to write. She handed me the note.

The guy in the yellow shirt and brown suit, that's Jason, it read.

I shrugged my shoulders as if to say who the hell Jason was... Yvette snatched the note from my hands, balled it up and proceeded to write another. She held the note in her two hands and turned it to me. The note said, *Jason Hill from high school....* It was written in all capital letters.

"Oh!" I mouthed silently.

Yvette shook her head up and down, balled up the note, let out a frustrated growl and began to write again.

Octavia, you don't remember him, she wrote.

I took another look at him, took her pen and sticky note and wrote back.

NO! I don't... Why should I remember him, did I fuck him?

No stupid, I did. She wrote back.

You're asking me to remember some guy from high school that meant absolutely nothing to me? Hell, I can barely remember half the guys I fucked in high school. How does she expect me to remember some twenty year old random fuck of hers?

Yvette started writing again. *I dated him in high school.*

I looked away from the note and across the sea of big hats and prayer cloths to the good looking brother in the brown suit. I looked back at Yvette with an agreeing nod and whispered a sarcastic, "And?"

Sister Johnson and her hat turned around again but before she could say a word we beat her to the punch and spontaneously put our finger to our lips and "Shhhhhhed" her. She rolled her big eyes and big ass hat around with that 'well I never' look. At this point, I had quite enough of Yvette's little guessing game and snatched her pen and sticky note pad and wrote:

Get to the effen point girl, 'cause you, Sister Johnson, and that dude in the brown suit are working my last nerve. Yaw'l gonna make me lose my religion up in here.

Yvette twisted her cinnamon brown colored glossy soup coolers to one side, sucked her teeth and giggled. She took the pen and sticky note pad from me and wrote.

I told him I was pregnant in high school and he gave me four hundred and fifty dollars for an abortion and you and I went shopping.

I wrote back. *Say word?*

She shook her head yes.

Well, were you pregnant? I wrote.

"No stupid," she blurted out loud.

Sister Johnson's hat turned halfway around, "Shhhhh Shhhhh Shhhhhh."

We tried to get back into the service, but we were both preoccupied. Pastor Clark preached on and a couple of Amen's later, the Pastor announced that we were now going to have a selection from our choir.

Just when the choir director raised her hands to the choir to lead them in song, Yvette nudged me and passed me a note.

I'm going to tell him the truth and apologize, the note said.

My eyes widened as I snapped my head back in Yvette's direction.

"WHAT," I said out loud.

Yvette shushed me and nodded her head yes. I took her paper and began to write.

Are you nuts? Hell! That was what, ten years ago? He probably doesn't remember it or you. She wrote back, *I'm gonna do it anyway, to clear my conscience.*

I wrote, *Are you serious? For ten years you've had a case of the fuck its and your conscience hasn't bugged you in all this time, all of a sudden you see him and you've got a case of morals. Bitch please!*

She wrote, *Just something I have to do, the truth shall set you free."*

I wrote, *Well gotta do what you gotta do.*

Yvette smiled at me, stood up and began to sing and clap along with the choir.

I began to think God touched this girl and urged her to clean her soul with the whole truth shall set you free thing. Shit, the truth can get you a black eye. I wanted to talk her out of it but she seemed to be at peace with her decision so I kept any further comments to myself.

After the church announcements and the offering, Pastor Clark gave the benediction and the congregation began greeting each other with hugs, kisses and praises of the Lord. Sister Johnson walked around the pew to me. Yvette made a beeline across the church to confess to Jason.

Sister Johnson gave me a big 'glad to see you came today' hug and called me Yvette. People are always getting us mixed up. I don't even correct them anymore. Then she scolded me for not seeing me for almost two years. I was tuning her out as I watched my sister sashay her blue dress over to Jason, shake his hand and sit down.

Sister Johnson kissed me on the cheek and made me promise to come back soon, then she reminded me the Devil only wants to destroy me and how I ought to give my life to the Lord before it's too late. She made a feeble attempt to wipe the makeup off of my shirt that she left there and walked away.

From her mouth to God's ears, I thought. *It may already be too late.*

Sister Johnson turned around, pointed her finger and demanded, "Bring that Octavia with you."

"Will do," I respectfully responded, then turned my attention back to Yvette and Jason. I tried to read the look on Jason's face as his expression changed from Damn it sure is nice to see you to what the hell did this bitch just say to me?

I watched them thinking that at this moment how much I admired Yvette, and respected her for doing what she was doing. Knowing flat out that this was something I could never do. I would have taken that secret to the grave. I'd probably burn in Hell, but it would save me a whole lot of humiliation now. Admit I lied? Never!

She's making me re-think my situation. I'm a woman in love with a man and involved with someone else and his seed is growing in my womb. I could never tell Calvin the baby's not his and how do I tell Lynn he's the father.

At this moment, Yvette was my She-Ro but I may need a superhero if Calvin finds out. Someone that can catch bullets with their teeth, leap tall buildings in a single bound with me on his back, and jump in between me and Calvin at the speed of light when Calvin tries to kill me.

I stood over a pew full of balled up sticky note papers that I had began to pick up and stick in my Coach bag to throw away later. Yvette walked back over to where we had sat, smiling.

"What's on your blouse," she asked. "Sister Johnson's face?"

"You ready to go," she asked, as if what she had just done was nothing. She wrapped her arm around mine as we walked toward the exit.

"Yeah I'm ready," I answered.

"Well, come on then," she said in her usual playful manner. "I feel like a weight has been lifted off my chest," she added.

"Yvette, you told him?"

"Yup."

"Well, what did he say?"

"He said he couldn't believe after all this time, I thought to do that. He said that he forgives me and then he asked for his four hundred and fifty dollars back."

"You gonna give it to him," I asked.

"I said I felt better, not stupid."

We laughed at the same time, the way twins freakishly do.

NOT.

I guess confession was good for the soul.

Chapter 8

I didn't sleep at all last night. It was a mixture of excitement and fear. I was going to see Lynn today. What do I say? He should be happy, he doesn't have any children.

However, we never discussed children. God knows I want a child.

I knew I looked tired. I couldn't get this bitter taste out of my mouth and my stomach was doing nasty things. My diet for the past two days had consisted of crackers, seltzer water and Tums but nothing was helping. This morning sickness has got me praying to the porcelain God every time I smell food.

I was trying to act normal so Calvin wouldn't question my sickness. I don't even want to tell him I'm pregnant yet, not until I spoke with Lynn.

Today, Lynn's friend Ron is having a cook out and I am expected to be there. Pulling my head off my pillow is hard. Calvin is getting up to go to a basketball game with his boy Turner. The phone rang, I manage to turn over to check the caller ID and saw the name M, TURNER.

I yelled to Calvin with everything in me to get the phone. Calvin was in the kitchen as I dragged myself in the kitchen for a cup of hot tea. It seemed as if his conversation changed. It sounded very familiar, quiet and evasive.

Yeah, huh and okays were no real conversation. Sounds just like the sneaky conversations I have with Lynn.

"Who is that" I asked.

Calvin looked at me and said to the person on the other end of the phone, "Man, let me go."

"Who was that," I asked as I sipped my hot tea.

"It was Turner, why you trippin?"

Maybe I was paranoid because of all the sneaky shit I've done.

"Why you whispering," I asked.

"Wasn't nobody whispering, 'Tavia," he said teasingly as he walked over and kissed me on the forehead. I felt my stomach go in reverse and I took a mad dash for the bathroom with Calvin right on my heels.

"You okay, babe?" He asked as he held my hair back and wiped my forehead.

I shook my head yes and let the wind out of my cheeks, scared to talk because the nausea was getting the best of me. It felt like every time I spoke, I would throw up.

"Maybe you should call your Doctor; you've been battling the flu for a couple of weeks now. You even look like you've lost a few pounds."

I sat on the bathroom floor laying my face on the side of the toilet for the coolness. I was panting like a dog.

"Maybe you should stay home today. I'll call you after the game to check on you before I go to work."

"Are you going straight to work from the game," I asked between pants.

"Yeah," he said as he kissed me on the forehead and said, "I'm out, feel better."

I got up, got myself together and cursed his uncaring ass out. Basketball takes precedence over everything. It always has.

Before I headed to Long Island, I called my Doctor.

"Hi Stephen, it's Octavia." I said when the doctor answered the phone.

"Hey 'Tavia, how are you feeling? I was worried about you because of the way you walked out of here. It concerned me. I tried calling you. Calvin didn't tell you?"

"No he didn't, did you tell him I was pregnant?"

"You know I wouldn't do that, not with the problems you guys have been having. You know I understand."

He had no idea why I might not want him to know about the baby. He didn't know half of what was going on. Stephen and I had a strange relationship. We talk a lot about personal things but I couldn't tell him the baby wasn't Calvin's. I was too embarrassed to admit my infidelity created a life and that I wasn't using condoms.

"Stephen, is it normal to feel like you're dying?"

"What do you mean?"

"I've thrown up three times already this morning and a few times last night, the smell of food makes me sick. I sipped on a cup of tea earlier to settle my stomach and it didn't help."

"Oh 'Tavia, tea was the worst thing you could have done. The caffeine is what made you sick."

He continued. "Octavia, morning sickness is part of the pregnancy package. Instead of eating three big meals, try six smaller portions. If it gets worst I'll prescribe you something, okay?"

"Alright," I agreed

"And no more caffeine," he demanded.

"No problem," I replied. "How are you and the wife getting along?"

"You know Pat is Pat, still bitchy and still selfish. I have had it with her bull but we'll talk about it later, I have patients waiting."

"Ok, but take care of yourself! You looked a little depressed when I saw you last," I said.

"Well when it came to spouses, you and I both picked winners," he pointed out.

"Don't I know it! Maybe we should hook Pat up with Calvin."

"Maybe we should, he said as we both laughed and hung up.

I love talking to Stephen. He's like a therapist and he's always there to talk when I need an ear. I'm his confidant. He tells me all about his family issues and his wife's infidelities.

***

I jumped on the highway to head to Long Island to meet Lynn. My stomach was churning; nausea and fear mixed up my gut. What do I say? How will he respond?

Well only one way to find out, I thought to myself as I was pulling off of exit 39, which was Glen Cove Road. I pulled into the parking lot at the Olive Garden where I was set to meet Lynn for our rendezvous.

My stomach began to knot in anticipation as I noticed his car. I suddenly became overwhelmed with happiness. I'm pregnant with his child, the man I'm madly in love with. I'm sure he'll be just as happy as I am.

"He has to be," I said out loud as I tried to convince myself.

I pulled my truck up alongside his car as he flashed me that pearly smile, obviously glad to see me. I jumped out to greet him and he hugged me like he missed me. I inhaled to take in the scent of him and everything seemed beautiful and perfect again. He took a step back and looked at me.

"You look different today," he stated as he grabbed my face with both hands and kissed my lips softly with slow pecks. My knees were weak, damn it, this man has a way with me.

He took my car keys from my hand, walked me over to the passenger side door of my truck, opened it and motioned for me to sit down. He closed the door behind me, leaned in the window and kissed my neck. I felt the warm air of his breath on my ear.

"Damn girl, I love your ass, you know that?"

"I know," I answered watching him walk in front of the truck to the driver's side and thinking to myself, *I really hope you do, baby, 'cause I'm about to drop a big ass bomb on you.*

We drove off hand in hand. I could see the Olive Garden get smaller and smaller in the passenger side mirror as we got further away from it. I got lost in thought.

"You're awfully quiet today, you okay?"

"Yeah I'm fine, just thinking."

"Thinking 'bout what," and before I could answer he cut me off.

"Did you get your period," he asked, taking his eyes off the road and putting them on me.

"Wha–Wha - What," I stammered and stuttered over my words.

"Diiiiid Yooou Geeeeet Yoooour PERIOD," he shouted over the music.

"Why did you ask that?" I said with a little giggle trying to lighten the mood. I didn't know how to respond to his question or his sarcasm.

"Because you haven't mentioned one these past few months."

"Oh," I responded. "As a matter of fact, I".... he cut me off and then he turned the radio off. His tone and demeanor completely changed as he let go of my hand and placed his on the steering wheel.

"Well, you know the only thing I want to hear from a woman is, guess what I did today." He continued.

"What," I said in a low tone, trying to fight back tears and without even looking at me, he said it again and real slow as if I was reading his lips. He went on pronouncing every word.

Theeeee Oooonly Thiiiiiiing IIIIIIIIIIII Waaaaant Tooooo Heeeaaar Frooooom

AAAAAAA Woooomaaaan Iiiiiiiiis

Guuueeeeeeess What the FUCK I did today! "Understand?"

Who the hell was this person sitting next to me? I've never seen this side of him. I was sick, the only response I had was, "Huh?"

"If you can huh, you can hear," he said in a stern, demanding voice.

I turned my head away from him to look out of the window so he couldn't see the tears that I could no longer hold back. For a few minutes, there was complete silence. Not even the traffic around us dared to make a sound. Lynn's voice roared up like thunder and broke the silence. I jumped as his hand patted my leg. The tone of his voice turned back to normal.

"Besides, you wouldn't know if it were mine or your husband's," he said, adding insult to injury as he turned the radio back up twice as loud as it was before. I guess that means the conversation was over.

I put my shades on and closed my burning eyes, the sickness in my stomach felt like I was being stabbed as his words echoed in my head. I thought of our baby steadily growing in my womb and the nausea constantly reminding me of its existence. I took a deep breath as Lynn sung along with the radio as if nothing ever happened.

With each word from his lips, I could feel my heart breaking, I mustered up enough courage to respond and I reached up to turn the radio off. Lynn looked at me as if I pissed in his Corn Flakes, as we pulled up in Ron's driveway where he met us with a Corona in his hand. I put on a fake smile, kissed Ron on his cheek and relieved him of that Corona.

God knows I need a drink. Good thing Ron's bar was fully stocked. I helped myself to a little bit of everything. I deserved an Oscar for the act I put on. I sat under Lynn's arm with him rubbing my neck as he laughed and joked with his boys. I was the only woman there besides Ron's mother, who asked where I was from.

"New Rochelle," I responded

"Where is that, in Jersey?" Ron's mother inquired.

"No, actually it's only about twenty or thirty minutes from here in Westchester County and ten minutes from Connecticut."

"And you come all the way down here to see him," she said pointing in Lynn's direction. I just smiled as Lynn responded.

"I have made the trip in this direction for years."

"How did you two meet? Long Island and New Rochelle are like two different sides of the earth. I never even heard of New Rochelle until today."

"We met at a club in the Bronx, Act III on strip night about six or seven years ago."

"You're a stripper," she uttered, sounding really shocked.

"Hell no," Lynn answered laughing. "It was a male review."

"And what the hell were you doing there?" Ron's mother pried.

"Nah, me and my boys were hanging in the Bronx and drove past that spot and there were a bunch of woman outside so we decided this must be the spot. I saw Octavia sitting in the back of the club half sleep at a table by herself so I asked her could I keep her company."

He continued on. "And as we were talking a guy walked up to her in a pair of pin striped dress pants, a bow tie and suspenders and asked was she ready to go, she shook her head yes. She got up and commenced to putting on her coat and gloves. The Mr. Bentley look alike walked back towards the door and I asked her if that was her man."

"She laughed at me and explained that he was her designated driver. I gave her my number and placed it close to her heart. The rest is history."

Yeah his story is right. I remembered the same events but my memory starred Mr. Perfect, not this stranger that sits next to me now, I thought to myself.

I sat silently listening and staring in his chestnut eyes wondering how we even got here in our relationship in the first place. It was just sex for a long time and then one day I woke up in love with him.

"She was in my life long before Nadia," he announced proudly.

Ron's mother gave him a wide eyed gaze as she snapped her head back like she couldn't believe he said that.

Lyyyyyynn," she said through closed teeth.

"Oh, 'Tavia knows about Nadia."

"You do," she said, looking at me for confirmation.

"Yeah, I do," I echoed.

"Well, how come you two aren't a couple," she asked. "That Nadia is a bitch, I don't like her. I don't even know why he's with her," She went on and on like she couldn't wait to get that out.

"Cause Tavia didn't want me," Lynn replied.

"What do you mean she didn't want you? She's here, isn't she?"

"She found someone better and married him on me. She came to her senses and came back to her man but that's okay, I still love her."

"I can tell. And I can also tell you love him too, it shows on your face. You two should just get it together and find a way to be together. It's obvious even to a duck you can't stay away from one another."

I thought so too. And I also thought this baby would make it easier for us to be together but who asked me to think? I saw this going differently in my head, I saw a happily ever after in my future.

I tried to get my mind off of our situation but I couldn't stop thinking about what he said because I could have kicked myself for not being strong enough to say something other than Huh.

I got up from the table feeling as if I was going to throw up every time he touched me. How could he sit here laughing and joking with his boys after breaking my heart?

He patted me on my ass as I walked past. I leaned down and whispered to Ron trying not to interrupt their conversation.

"Where's the bathroom?"

"Through the kitchen, it's the first door on the left."

I double timed to the bathroom so I wouldn't throw up all over the place and just in the nick of time. I turned the bathroom faucet on to drown out the sound of my heaves. I don't know if it was the pregnancy, the mixed liquors or his evil double personality that was making me sick. But I felt as if I was throwing up my soul.

I just broke down and cried like a baby, my chest started to hurt and I couldn't catch my breath. My legs abandoned me as I slid down the wall and sat on the floor with my head between my legs and hugged myself.

There was a knock on the door.

"You fall in?"

"No, I'll be out in a sec."

I put my mouth under the faucet and took a sip, put a little toothpaste in my mouth to mask the smell of vomit, then I splashed a little on my face trying to compose myself but my eyes were blood shot.

I sat there on the toilet seat for a few minutes trying to gain my composure when there was a second knock. I opened the door and Ron was standing there.

"Damn girl, look at your eyes they're all red and swollen. You ok?"

"I'm fine," I damn near knocked him down getting back in the bathroom to throw up again.

"Whoa! You had too much to drink, huh?" He held back my hair and rubbed my back. "You need some water or something?"

"Yes, please."

I sat back down and held my now throbbing head. I always get a headache when I cry. Ron handed me a glass of cold water and patted my forehead with a damp washcloth.

"I'll go get Lynn for you," he said.

I grabbed his hand. "Please don't!" I whispered. "I'll be okay."

"Are you sure? You don't look good."

"No really, I'm okay," I said as a tear ran down my face.

"What's that about? Is there trouble in paradise?" Ron asked me.

More tears followed. Ron put his arms around me. I laid my tear drenched cheek on his throwback.

"What's the matter, 'Tav? You're always so happy. Don't cry, did your husband do something to you? You know that nigga can be dealt wit'."

I shook my head no.

"Did Lynn do something?"

Again, I shook my head no.

"Well what's wrong," he asked, insisting on an answer.

"I can talk to you, right?"

"No doubt, girl! You know you my people. What? You got a bun in the oven?"" he said, trying to lighten the mood.

I shook my head again, but this time up and down.

"Yo, you're pregnant?" His voice changed to a higher excited pitch. He jumped out of my reach. "Word," he said with a laugh. "Does Lynn know?"

Again, I shook my head no.

"You gonna tell him?"

I shrugged my shoulders. "I don't know," I said as I sniffed the snot running out my nose. "I haven't told him yet, I just found out a few days ago. I've been trying to figure out a way to break it to him."

"What do you mean break it to him? You're about to break it off with him?"

Just then, I heard Lynn's voice.

"Yo man, you trying to steal my girl," he said jokingly.

"Yo Lynn, she's sick, I think you need to take her home." Ron informed him.

"Babe, you alright," he asked, sounding sincere. Out of concern his fingers began moving through my hair which was matted to my forehead from sweating.

"I'm okay, just had too much to drink" I said as I looked over at Ron.

"I'll go get your purse, okay?" As he walked out, I grabbed Ron's arm.

"Please don't tell him," I begged. "I'm trying to find the right time."

"Don't worry about it, mums the word. You just feel better and I'm sure Lynn will be okay with whatever your decision is."

"Thanks for everything." Ron just nodded his head. As we drove off Ron yelled, "Tavia tell your Doublemint twin to call me."

I threw my hand out the window in acknowledgment.

Lynn drove back to the Olive Garden where he left his car, rubbing my head all the way. "You alright, sexy?"

"Yeah, I'm fine."

"Can you drive home or do you need me to drive you home?" Lynn asked me.

"No, I'm good to drive," I said, trying to sound cheerful as he kissed me on the forehead like everything was all grits and gravy.

"All right," he said as he got out of my car and into his. "Call me when you get home," he shouted.

I rehearsed over and over again what I was going to say to him when I called. I can't believe how cold he was. I was devastated, who was that man? I turned my cell phone off and rode around for hours rubbing my belly and crying until I could barely catch my breath.

I cried until no more tears would come. What does he mean the only thing he wants to hear is guess what I did today? Those cold words played over and over in my head like a broken record.

I guess I'll go home and bury my head under a pillow and feel sorry for my damn self and have a nice little pity party.

***

I walked in the door all the lights were on, I knew Calvin was still home. He should be getting up to go to work soon. I figured I'd just climb in next to him and try not to wake him. There was an 8x10 size piece of paper on the comforter next to him that read, PLEASE WAKE

ME UP AND FUCK ME in black magic marker and all capital letters with a big happy face drawn on it.

Oh hell no, I thought to myself. I put the note back on the bed, grabbed a sheet out of the linen closet and crashed on the sofa. I was awakened two hours later by the door slamming and Calvin cursing. "Shit, I'm late for work," he shouted. "You could have woken me up!"

I don't give a damn how he's feeling right now, he just wanted some butt. I'm sick of him, sick of Lynn and just plain fuckin' sick. I got up and climbed in my now empty bed hugging my pillow and rewinding the last six months in my head and asking myself why.

I finally gathered what I was going to say to him when I spoke to him; I just had to find the courage to say it. My mother always said that if you ever want to get rid of a man ask him for money or tell him you're pregnant.

Chapter 9

I woke up feeling like I had lost my best friend, my body's little intruder had me running straight to the bathroom no sooner than I opened my eyes. I noticed Calvin hadn't come home this morning. He's probably at his mother's house complaining about me. That ought to make her day, she can't stand me anyway. I was never light enough for her, she's very color struck and wants high yellow grandbabies. That's funny coming from a woman that's not that damn light herself.

I had a moment of clarity and I made up my mind. I've tried for so long to have a baby; Lynn's just going to have to deal with it. He can't tell me what to do with my body, I tried to convince myself. I wasn't being selfish but I just couldn't see myself in the chop shop.

Lynn was about to see a whole new side of me. Since he's known me he's gotten the watered-down, diluted version of Octavia because he had no reason to see the bitch. My door bell downstairs rings my phone, so I answered it.

"Who?"

"Your mirror image," the voice shouted back. The voice on the other end of the phone sounds just like mine so I buzzed her up.

"What's going on, Mi-Mi?"

"Not a thing, You-You." That's what we used to call each other when we were young, since we were identical she would call me mi and I would call her you.

That used to drive our mother nuts because even she could hardly tell us apart most of the time. And since we never called each other by name it was hard to figure out if you sat around waiting for her to call me Octavia and me to call her Yvette.

She used to say, "You look just like me."

My reply was, "Yeah, I look just like you."

Yvette began to rummage through my fridge.

"Damn, your fridge looks like mine! Are our refrigerators twins, too?"

"Yeah bitch! It's empty! So, what you got planned today?"

"Not a thing! Oh before I forget, Ron said give him a call."

"Sho'nuff. Hell, the way you talk about Lynn, if the sex is anything like that I'll be following your ass to Long Island."

"Yeah, if he's anything like Lynn," I mumbled.

"You know what they say birds of a feather."

"Huh," I exhaled.

"What's that about?"

"Nothing, just hungover," I answered.

"I came by to use your fax machine, Mi-Mi. You listen to Wendy Williams on WBLS in the afternoon, right?"

"Yeah at 2 pm. Well, most of the time, but I listen to Michael Baisden on Kiss for Love, Lust and Lies."

"I just faxed Wendy a letter telling her about my confession in Church. I wonder if she's gonna read it on the air?"

"You did what, girl, you'll be embarrassed!"

"I sent it anonymously, so listen to her show today and tell me if she reads it."

"I'll be at work, alright?"

My sister gave me an idea. I'll fax Wendy about my situation just to get her opinion, and get this off my chest.

Dear Wendy,

I'm a 27 year old woman from New Rochelle. I've been married to a wonderful man for a few years who just doesn't do it for me sexually. So, I've been holding down a secret lover even longer than I've been married. We've been sneaking off for secret rendezvous' three or four days out of every week when my husband is at work. My true dilemma is I'm pregnant and guess who's not the father? That's right, the husband. The day I went to tell my jump off, to whom I was ready to leave my husband for, he asked me when was the last time I got my period? Wendy, before I could answer and give him what I thought was good news, he did a Doctor Jekyll and Mr. Hyde on me and said you better not be pregnant 'cause the only thing I want to hear from a woman is guess what I did today.

Wendy, I was so sick that I couldn't say anything. I never saw this side of him before. And I damn sure didn't see that coming. Now, I don't believe in abortions so I'm keeping my baby. So should I tell the jump off in spite of his comment or should I break it off with him and raise this baby as my husband's and take my secret to the grave? I

already know what I'm going to do, I guess I just wanted to tell somebody to get it off my

chest and not take my secret to the grave.

Sincerely,

Your friend in my head

I feel like I just went to confessions at church and I'm not going to listen to Wendy today just in case she reads my fax because I don't want to hear her tell me how deceitful and irresponsible I was being and how raunchy I was being for not making my jump off use protection and letting him splash off in me. She'll probably tell me I should be a woman about my shit, leave them both, tell the father and raise my bastard child on my own. And she'd be right; I just don't want to hear it.

Half the day has gone by and I haven't heard from Lynn which was unusual. Normally, I would have spoken to him twice already before three o' clock. I listened to WBLS today because Michael Baisden's Love, Lust and Lies mimicked my life.

If I didn't have so much lust, I wouldn't have told so many damn lies and I wouldn't have fallen in love with the man that slayed me sexually. I can't catch a goddamn break. I turned the radio off and called Calvin's cell but I got no answer so I called my mother in law's house.

"Hello," she answered with her thick West Indian accent.

"Hi Mama Michaels, is my husband there?" She paused for a minute leaving me listening to dead air.

"Hello!!!" I shouted into the phone.

"I'm here dear, you don't have to shout. No, my son is not here. Who is this, Makin she asked, trying to be funny.

Makini is the woman she wished her son married, a very high yellow girl. However, she knew damn well who it was, how many women was her son married to. But I stayed polite trying not to lose my temper and exercise some self-restraint.

"No Mom Michaels, its Octavia."

"How can I help you?"

"Well, if you see your son, my husband, can you ask him to call me?"

"You'll be home," she asked with a sarcastic undertone.

"Yes I will," I snapped back at her. The next thing I heard was a dial tone. That rude obnoxious hag hung up on me.

I know she's not going to tell him I called. To be honest, I don't know why I called. I guess I was feeling sorry for myself and I wanted some comforting.

I put my Fantasia CD on repeat and played Free Yourself over and over again. I fell asleep and woke up to the sound of Fantasia's voice and the phone ring along with it.

My voice was raspy and groggy. "Yes," I answered as I cleared my throat.

"Hi Octavia, it's me Lynnwood."

Hmmmm, he was not his usual perky self and all of a sudden he was being so formal. Oh, my heart instantly sank and my stomach began to do the butterfly dance.

"That's it, huh? What happened to hi baby, hello, love of my life?"

What happened to the terms of endearment that signified our relationship? Now there's just tension and nervousness.

"Octavia, why is talking to you today like pulling teeth?"

" Talking to you is just as painful, though." I admitted.

"What's that supposed to mean?"

Duly noted, I noticed he was putting up his defenses. "Nothing."

"Don't lie to me, 'Tav."

"Lie to you? You know I can't stand a liar." He must have forgotten the shit he said to me last night. Men have the ability to be complete assholes.

They say whatever they feel like saying, don't care if your feelings get hurt and then blame all the bullshit on you. I swear there must be a class given to all men at birth on how to be a complete idiot 101 and a refresher course given in junior high in the boys' gym.

There must be a pusher giving away idiot juice and all those dick carrying mother fuckers took a sip.

I can't believe Lynn is acting this way. I have to tell him how I feel.

Just as I geared up to let him have it he said, "I know you hate liars so I better tell you this now, Nadia is getting married."

"Nadia's getting married to who," I questioned as I straightened my posture in the bed.

"Well, I told her if she came up with a certain amount of money, I'd marry her." I was silent. I couldn't speak. His words were like a grenade going off and shrapnel hit me everywhere.

"Tavia, say something."

"What do you want me to say?"

"I don't know. Say something, anything! Just speak to me."

"Is she pregnant?"

"Noooooo." Lynn answered.

"Well, how? Why? How could you?"

"Octavia, it's not such a big deal. Nothing has to change."

"Are you crazy, everything has changed," I shouted, moving the phone away from my ear and in front of my face like a microphone.

"Octavia, Octavia," he repeated. "Shh, stop yelling. Calm down."

He wants me to calm down. He just asked me to say something, anything and now that I did he wants me quiet. "I thought you told me you would never marry that bitch."

"Look 'Tavia, that bitch is going to be my wife."

He's defending her? Since when was he doing that? He usually acts like he can barely stand the sight of her.

I gathered some courage and reluctantly asked, "When is this blessed affair supposed to take place?"

"Soon."

"How soon is soon?"

"The 30th!"

"Of this month?"

"Yeah." Lynn answered.

"That's only two weeks away."

"I do love you, Octavia."

The tears began to flow. I tried not to sound too hurt so I stopped talking, mainly because I couldn't breathe. I'm carrying his child and *she* gets the man. He led me to believe he would never marry her, he said it wasn't that serious.

My head began to pound and no more words would come out. The storm working its way up through my stomach had erupted. I dropped the phone and ran for the bathroom and I didn't make it. I fell to my knees and crawled to the bathroom. I curled up in the fetal position, overwhelmed with grief. I couldn't get the will to move or to pull myself up. The stench of vomit on my shirt and the floor smothered me and weakened my stomach even more.

I jumped in the shower to wash the pain away. I stood under the hot water sobbing until the walls started to sweat and the feeling of claustrophobia took over me as if the walls were closing in on me. My heart was breaking and I can't stop loving this man. I keep visualizing him in a tux saying "I do". It kept repeating on me like bad shrimp. How could he hurt me like this?

Oh God help me, I was realizing that our whole relationship was a lie.

I lay in my bed unable to move. I watched the 48 hour marathon of Good Times. I remember this episode when Thelma married Keith, the man of her dreams. He could have had any woman he wanted and he chose her. It was the fairytale wedding. Keith was in his tux and Thelma was being walked down the aisle in her beautiful white dress being given away by her brother to the man she loves. Michael sang a heartwarming rendition of *You and I*.

Jealousy filled me and the reality of my situation hit me like a ton of bricks. Nadia was marrying the man of my dreams.

My phone rang, it was my sister.

"Hey girl, did you listen to the Wendy Williams Show today? Did she read my letter?"

"No 'Vette, I didn't."

"What's wrong?" She asked with a bit of concern in her voice.

"Nothing, why?" I lied.

"Come on girl, you can fool everybody else but we're twins so I can feel when something is wrong."

I began to sniffle and cry as I answered.

"Lynn is getting married." I said, between sniffs. "Oh girl, what am I gonna do?"

"Lynn's marrying who," she blurted.

"The –the - the the girl he's seeing."

"When did you find out?" My sister asked.

"Tonight."

"When is the wedding? Next summer?"

"This year."

"This year? What's the rush? Is she pregnant?"

"That's the same question I asked and he said no."

"You need me to come over there honey? I'm on my way!"

"No, no, please 'Vette. I just want to be by myself."

"Hell, we can go to Long Island and beat that hoe down. Then we can break his window, slash his tires, throw paint on his Expedition and key the hell out of his shit."

"That will make you feel better."

"Hell! It will make me feel better, hurt my little sister, I keep a gallon of paint and a bat in my truck for just the occasion."

Yvette carried on and on because she's very protective of me. Good thing I didn't tell her I was pregnant.

"Call that mu'fucka's house. I want to talk to him."

"No Yvette, let it go."

"See that's your fuckin problem right there! You're always letting shit go. Fuck that, fuck him and fuck that bitch he's about to marry. Call that nigga. You're too nice Mi-Mi, tooooo freakin nice. See, Lynn needs a bitch like me. I would blow his spot, show up at the wedding and show my black ass out."

"What should I do, 'Vette?"

"I told your ass what to do! Blow that nigga's spot."

"I love him and I don't want to hurt him in any way."

"You don't want to hurt *him*? You're sitting over there crying like someone just cut off your pinkies and you don't want to hurt *him*. Why not, you're hurt, right? You know what, give me Ron's number right now. I'm gonna call him. No, you call him on the three-way."

"Why?"

"I want to know why he didn't tell you if that's supposed to be your boy."

"Yeah well, he's Lynn's boy first."

"Whatever, call that nigga." My sister demanded.

"Okay, hold on." I clicked over, dialed his number and his girlfriend answered. "Hello, Hi Carol. It's Octavia, is Ron home?"

"Oh hi, Octavia. He's right here! Hold on, okay?"

I heard her whisper, "Lynn's still seeing her, she doesn't know?"

Then I heard Ron shush her then he got on the phone. "Hi Ron."

"Hey Tavia, are you feeling better?"

Before I could respond, my sister jumped in, "Why didn't you tell my sister Lynn was getting married?"

"Whoa, pump your breaks, lady. Who's that, Yvette?"

"Ya damn right."

"Hold up a minute. Octavia, that was none of my business."

"So you were just gonna let your man hurt her like that?"

"First of all ladies, Lynn led me to believe you knew and were ok with it."

"Well she didn't and she's not." My sister answered for me.

"Yo, yo why are you yelling at me? I don't like that chick he's marrying but he's got his reasons. I was hoping when you told him you were pregnant he would rethink his decision."

Oh Lord, why did he say that? I hadn't told Yvette yet. Here we go, Tick tick tick boom!

"WHAT! Octavia, you're pregnant?" My sister screamed.

"Yes," I answered like a child being chastised.

"Oh, hell no! You're getting rid of that lying ass nigga's baby, right?"

"Wait a minute," Ron interrupted. "Tavia, you didn't tell him?"

"Listen y'all, the reason I didn't tell him is because the day I found out he told me I better not be because the only thing he wanted to hear was guess what I did today."

"No he didn't," they both said. They both went on a tangent.

"Tell him, he needs to know," Ron yelled.

"No sis, don't tell him shit! Get rid of that headache and get rid of him," Yvette screamed.

"Tavia, you know what your problem is? You won't fight for what you want."

"My sister doesn't need him. She can work it out with her husband and forget about Lynn and forget about his bastard child."

"Or she can keep it, tell Lynn and live happily ever after." Ron countered.

"Get rid of it," Yvette repeated.

"Keep it," Ron exclaimed. "He'd want to know."

I felt like I was standing there with the devil on one shoulder and an angel on the other trying to persuade me to do their will.

"Look you two, I've got to figure this out for myself. I can't believe he's doing this."

"You ever think he may have told you because he wanted you to stop him, talk him out of it."

Yvette yelled, "Oh please, he's a dog."

I sat there picturing Yvette sitting there rolling her eyes, twirling her hair and popping off her silk wrapped nails.

"Octavia think about it, he could have gotten married and not told you. You would have never found out."

I waited for my witty ass sister's response to that but there was none. I could hear her huffing through the phone.

"You're right."

"Besides you were too good to him, you never told him no. You never cursed his ass out even when he was wrong. You let him take naked pictures of you when you had that threesome."

Oh hell, that time bomb was about to blow again.

"YOU DID WHAT?" Yvette screamed so loud, I had to move my ear from the phone. The silence was broken.

"Here we go." I said, sarcastically.

"Ya damn right, here we go. You had a threesome with that fuck? Ooooh girl, of all the dumb bone headed shit."

I screamed, interrupting her rant, "YVETTE! I know. Please not now, okay?"

"Oh, we're gonna fuck that nigga up."

"Now hold up, that's my man. I can't let that happen." Ron interrupted.

"Look both of you, it's my life and I've got to deal with it."

"So you're saying you don't want my help?"

"That's what I'm saying."

"Fine, bitch." The next thing I heard was a click.

"Did she hang up, 'Tavia?"

"Yeah, she did."

"Your sister is off the fuckin chain."

"Yeah she is, but she means well. She's extremely animated especially when it comes to me."

"Seriously Tav, you need to call Lynn tomorrow and talk to him. I know he loves you."

"I've got to worry about me and this baby right now."

"And you don't think Lynn needs to know?"

"No! He made his choice."

"See, that's your problem, you won't fight for what you want." Ron stated his earlier observation.

"Ron, it's a losing battle. I have too much pride to beg him. I can't believe he's going to marry her."

"What, you thought he was going to marry you?"

"No, no, no," I stuttered. "I just thought maybe we would be together."

"You could be, if you tell him."

"I don't think so, I gotta go."

"Yo, tell your sister to holla at me. I love those feisty mean chicks." Ron laughed.

"Yeah, Ron, whatever. I'll call you some other time."

I hung up with Ron and called my sister back. Her line was busy, I knew what that meant. Her phone was off the hook and she didn't want to talk to me anymore tonight, so I tried calling Calvin back.

I guess if you can't be with the one you love, love the one you're with. His phone rang, and then he picked up. There was loud music in the background and a lot of voices. I kept yelling, "Hello," and no one answered. The phone hung up, so I called back and it just rang and rang with no answer. I wonder what happened.

I really need him to hold me tonight. I figured I'd wait up for him. I lay down on the bed flicking through the channels.

The next thing I knew, it was morning and I heard Calvin's voice. He was talking on the phone in the other room so I pressed the speaker button on the fax machine to see who he was talking to. There was a woman's voice on the other line. They were talking about a car and something about a basketball game.

Then I heard Calvin say "Hold on, I think she's up."

I pressed the speaker button again to hang up and I played possum. I felt his presence in the bedroom then I felt the breeze of him as he walked back out of the room.

I pressed the button again.

Calvin said, "Naw, she's still sleep."

The female voice said, "Boy, you're crazy."

I hung up the phone and walked out to the kitchen where he was standing with his back to the door whispering and laughing. I stood there naked as the day I was born with my arms crossed over my tender breast. Calvin caught a glimpse of me out of the corner of his eye and jumped. His smile turned into a quick frown. "Shit Oc', you scared me."

"Oh, did I?"

He turned to his phone call and said, "Let me go, I think I'm in trouble."

He hung up the phone and said, "What's the problem?"

"Where have you been, I've been trying to call you. I haven't seen you in two days. I called your mother's house and your cell."

"What did my mother say?"

"That you weren't there." I snapped.

"I was in the Village playing ball."

"For two whole days?"

"No, not for two days. Look, this is what happened."

Here we go, I thought. Anytime you hear 'this is what had happened', brace yourself because you are in for some bullshit.

I'm gonna listen and give him this one because of all my bull.

He continued, "I was playing ball in the East Village and got kneed in the head. My shit was pounding and I could hardly see out of my right eye. This guy gave me an aspirin and I don't remember anything after that. I woke up in his place in my boxers alone and locked in the apartment."

I've known this man for over eight years and he's never, *I mean never* taken an aspirin, not even when he had a toothache. Now he's sitting here with a straight face trying to con me into believing he took an aspirin from a stranger he met on the basketball court in the East Village.

Come on, you can't cheat a cheater but I let him go on with his story before I interjected.

"So why didn't you call the police," I asked.

"There was no phone in the place and I couldn't get a signal on my cell."

"Really, how'd you get out?" I asked, basking along in his lies.

"The guy came home. When he came in, I ran out."

"Do you feel like you had sex?"

"I KNEW YOU'D THINK THAT SHIT," he yelled, flying off the handle. "You're always thinking somebody's cheating."

What the hell was he talking about? There was only one other time and I didn't accuse him of anything. I never accused him of cheating; the thought never crossed my mind. Me and my selfish ass was so busy doing me. I didn't stop to think he might be doing someone else.

That song, *Who's Making Love To Your Old Lady* by Johnnie Taylor came to mind. But I guess I deserve that one. He gets a free coochie coupon because he's about to raise the next man's baby so I dropped the subject.

"How are you feeling now? Are you all right? You need something?" I asked, sounding like the caring wife as I rubbed his head. Deep down, I knew that was the guilty wife speaking.

"I love you baby," he said. Let's not fight."

"I don't want to fight Cal, I was just worried."

He kissed me and began to undress as he fondled my breast and pulled me on to the carpet while touching and rubbing me.

I thought to myself, *I'm so stupid. I cheated on a good man and almost left him for a man that clearly didn't love me.* But I still loved Lynn. I couldn't bring myself to hate him. Calvin whispered in my ear, "You know I'd never cheat on you." I shut my eyes and pretended he was Lynn.

He whispered, "I want you," and a tear rolled down my face as I imagined it to be Lynn inside of me.

"Please honey, make love to me. Please, I need you."

***

Calvin wasn't making love to me. He fucked me like a wild animal. When he slapped my ass, he slapped it so hard that it hurt. He thrusted hard and fast like he was just working for that nut and just as I suspected he shook violently, grunted and slumped over on top of me.

I laid underneath him staring at the ceiling, tears streaming from both eyes and finding themselves in puddles in my ears. My stomach was acting up and I couldn't breathe from his dead weight on my chest. Lynn was still on my mind.

Calvin climbed off me, jumped in the shower and called to me. I went in the bathroom, sat on the toilet in a feeble attempt to squeeze his deposit out of me and answered him. "Yes, honey?"

"Sorry I came so quickly, but you know it's been a while and you know your coochie's good like that."

Oh please, he always cums quick. What makes today any different, I thought to myself.

I just smiled as if I believed what he was saying.

"I need you to do me a favor."

"Okay, what do you need?"

"I can't get the weekend off and this is the week my mom is moving to Virginia. I need you to drive the moving truck down for me."

"Oh come on Cal, you know your mom doesn't like me."

"She likes you baby. I can't do it, so do it for me, okay?"

"No, she doesn't like me." I insisted.

"Where did you get an idea like that?"

"You told me that I wasn't yellow enough, remember?"

"That's when we first got together."

"I haven't gotten any lighter over the years."

"I know, 'Tavia. But do me this favor."

"All right, all right, when am I leaving?" I said, giving into his pleading.

"Thursday, I'll pay for your bus ticket to come back Monday morning. Why don't you bring your sister with you for company? I'll pay her bus fare too."

"Yeah, I just might." I knew Yvette was hot with me right now but maybe she'd take that ride.

Chapter 10

It's 95 degrees out tonight but it feels like one hundred and five. The New Jersey Turnpike smells like a can of open ass. It's fuckin up my already twisted stomach. If you roll up the window and turn on the AC, the odor comes through the vents.

This U-haul sounds like it's going to break down every time I turn the air conditioner on, so I kept it off. I felt like I was melting. Yvette took the ride with me, even though she's still not talking to me and the radio in the U-haul didn't work once we got out of New York.

To make matters worse, there was no tape deck or CD player either so the seven hour drive to Richmond was long. It was just me, my pissed off sister's along with her attitude, the heat, this raggedy ass truck, my broken heart and disturbing thoughts.

And on top of everything else, I'm about to spend the next three days with a woman that hates my black ass.

"You want me to drive," Yvette asked, breaking the silence.

"No, I'm alright," I had my thoughts to keep me awake.

Yvette insisted though so I pulled over at the Maryland House and let her take over. We followed the directions straight to her door and arrived at four A.M.

We crashed out in the truck until sun up and my Mother In-Law gracefully woke us up by banging on the hood of the U-haul.

She walked over to Yvette and said, "Oh, you brought your sister with you" with a little attitude in her tone.

She likes Yvette even less than she likes me. The first day I brought 'Vette over to her house to pick up Calvin, we overheard her tell Calvin to watch my sister because she may steal.

This woman is a piece of freakin work.

"No she brought me with her, I'm Yvette." She corrected her.

"You two look so much alike that I can't tell who's who. Can Calvin tell you apart? You could actually switch mates and no one would be the wiser."

What the hell was she trying to imply? Yvette was about to rip her a new one. I grabbed her arm before she could speak, "Relax 'Vette, she's just an old miserable lady."

"Yo Tavia for real, I don't know how you put up with that shit. I'll fight an old lady. It's hard to believe Calvin is her son, you know she's poisoning his mind every chance she gets."

"I married him, not her. I don't care what she says."

Mrs. Michaels was already going through her belongings in the back of the truck. She just started unloading and giving orders.

About an hour later, I saw a Volvo pull up. It was one of Calvin's sisters. She came to help her mother get moved in. She lives in Maryland. Yvette sat there popping off her silk wraps. It's something she does when she gets annoyed.

"Hey Octavia. Hey Yvette."

"Hi Janelle," we both answered.

"My brother couldn't come?"

"No, he had to work."

"Thank you for driving this stuff here."

"Not a problem, I needed a vacation."

"Tell me about it. I left Akil at home. I just wanted some time to myself."

"Girl, I feel you," Yvette added. "Everyone needs a break from their ball and chain."

Janelle recruited four young guys from the area to help move the stuff in while Yvette demonstrated the true meaning of vacation. She sat on her ass and didn't do shit. The next day, it rained all day. The news said severe hurricane watch and lightning storms. Janelle decided to leave that day so she didn't get caught in the storm.

"Octavia, would you like to ride to Maryland with me and catch the bus from there? It will be cheaper."

"We get to leave early," Yvette sounded excited. "Hallelujah!"

"Sure thing," I answered. "When are we leaving?"

"In a few, I want to be back in Maryland before the storm hits. We can't get stuck here."

Yvette yelled out, "I'll wait in the car." She grabbed her bag and packed it in the car.

I bid my goodbyes and jumped in the backseat. Just as we hit I-95 North, the wind picked up blowing garbage across the highway. I went to sleep and woke up in Maryland right when we were pulling up in Janelle's yard.

There were three cars parked in her driveway, one was Akil's, the other was Janelle's truck and the third was unidentified.

"Whose car is this in my yard," Janelle yelled as she jumped out of the car and made a beeline in her house.

Yvette and I struggled to carry our bags inside but as soon as we got to the door some random becky ran past us putting on her shirt with her pants in her hand. She was bare ass, bare foot and running like hell. Janelle was running behind her throwing her shoe at her.

Janelle went back downstairs. Yvette and I just looked at each other in amazement but never said a word. We finally made our way into the living room where two of Akil's friends sat playing PlayStation. They were laughing their asses off until they saw us standing there.

You could hear yelling and screaming coming from downstairs and then silence. Just as Yvette and I sat down on the sofa, Akil oozed his ass up out of the basement brushing his hair with a smug look on his face.

"What up twins?" He greeted us.

"Hey!''

He walked out the front door and his video game playing posse followed.

Yvette turned to me, "WHAT the Fuck was that," she said with a nervous giggle.

"Girl that damn Akil didn't know she was coming home a day early and got busted. His ass brought a chick up in her house."

"And the moral of this lesson would be what," Yvette asked, jokingly.

"Call before you come home!"

***

Janelle was so hurt and embarrassed that she didn't come up from the basement until morning when she woke us up to get ready to leave. Akil was just dragging his sorry ass in from the night before. He walked in the house not even looking at Janelle, turned to us and said, "Gooooood morning, twins" and winked his eye.

"Heeeeey Akil."

That dude has got some kind of nerve and really doesn't give a fuck.

Janelle didn't say a word to him, she just walked out. "I'll be in the car when you girls are ready."

I felt so bad for her. I went to the car to see if she was ok.

"Don't tell my brother, okay."

"All right, I won't."

My sister came out and didn't say a word. She got in the car and huffed like someone did something to her.

"Now what's wrong with you," I asked.

Yvette just shook her head and looked out the window. We made it to the bus station just in time for the next bus to New York.

I kissed Janelle on the cheek and whispered, "Be strong."

My sister heard me and as we walked away she responded.

"Yeah, she's going to need to be strong living with that dog," she said, throwing away a piece of paper.

"What was that?" I asked, curiously.

"Akil's cell number, he slid it to me when you went to the car. He thought I was you. All up on my ass telling me he knows Calvin ain't fucking you right and how you needed a real man."

"What? Oh, he's sick and has no conscience. He didn't even care when he got caught."

"Tavia," her mood zoomed into serious. "What are you gonna do about the baby?"

"Yvette, I'm keeping it."

"Do what you think is best, I'm here for you. I love you," as she placed her hand in mine.

"I know Vette. I know and I love you too."

I looked out the window until the line in the road began to connect again. I started wondering when this wedding was going to take place playing in my head like a bad rerun. I guess he made my choice for me. He's marrying her and he doesn't want any kids. Calvin does so this plan is pretty mapped out. I'm just going to work out my marriage.

I called Stephen on his cell to schedule my ultrasound appointment and to talk to him about what's going on. I know I can always talk to him without judgment but I didn't get an answer. He always picks up his cell, I was thinking that maybe he went to the Poconos this weekend with his wife and daughter.

I guess things are better for them. I'm glad because he's a nice guy. I hope his marriage works out better than mine.

I looked over at Yvette, she was snoring and her head was rocking back and forth like a bobble head. Just as we were pulling into Grand Central Bus terminal, I woke her up. "Mi-Mi, wake up."

"Huh", she answered, wiping the slob off the side of her face.

"We're home." We got off the bus and caught the Metro North to New Rochelle.

"Yvette, you missed your stop."

"No, I'm going to mommy's house. I'm gonna see if she's gonna cook dinner. Besides, I left my car over there, did you forgot?"

"Yeah, I did. I'll come over there after I get settled in. I have to talk to Calvin."

"You know I got your back, right?" My sister said.

"All day, all night."

We called a Red Fox taxi. "Yeah, can I get a taxi to 33 Lincoln and then to 81 Winthrop?"

As Yvette got out of the cab she said, "I'll tell Ma you're coming."

I stepped in my apartment, not a light was on and I don't remember seeing Calvin's car in the parking lot. The bed hasn't been slept in. It's made and he never makes the bed. I started putting my things away when the phone rang.

"Octavia?" My younger brother's voice said.

"Yeah, Omar, what's up?"

"Mommy said when you come over to pick up today's paper."

"Okay, why what's up?"

"I'll put Mommy on."

"Hey baby," my mother said, sounding a little down.

"Hi Mama, what's wrong?"

"Are you sitting down?"

"I am now, what's wrong?"

"I was reading the paper today and there was an accident. They found a car on the Tappan Zee Bridge."

"Wait Mama, wait!" I held my stomach trying to control the nervous butterflies building up. "What happened?"

"The police found Stephen's body washed up on the Hudson. The newspaper said he abandoned his vehicle and jumped to his death."

"Oh my God! How, why? He made it seem as if things were getting better for him and his wife."

"Honey I'm sorry, I know he was your friend."

"That explains why he didn't answer his phone."

"Where were his daughter and wife?"

"According to the newspaper, they are at their other home in the Pocono Mountains."

"Mama, I got to go."

"Your sister said she's coming over to your house."

"No! Tell her I'll be over there as soon as I get in touch with Calvin."

I got off the phone feeling a little disorientated. What could make Stephen do a thing like that? I can't believe it. He said he wanted to talk and I wasn't here to talk to him. I have to call my mother back to see when this happened, I pressed redial forgetting that she had called me. But it rang and I got Calvin's voicemail.

I looked at the display window on the phone. It was Calvin's cell number followed by the numbers 22079. That's my birthday and then a series of one's and nines followed.

I figured out this must be his cell number code and the number ones were to listen to the messages and the nines were to save the message. So I pressed the code and then the number one to check his messages. The machine said that there were five saved messages.

"Cal sweetie, it's me, I just call to say I missed you." The answering machine prompted me to press seven to erase and nine to save. I pressed nine.

The second saved message was the same woman's voice, "Calvin Michaels," the voice said in a sweet tone. "You left your throwback over here yesterday, I can't wait for you to come back and get it."...... I thought he just had a casual tryst, this sounds serious. As I listened to the third message, "Are we still going to dinner while your wife's away?" I began to drift off thinking I've got to put a stop to this.....Next message, "Calvin, I missed you today, love you call me when you get the message"...."Hi Baby hope you didn't get in trouble for staying out all night again. Love you talk to you later." By this time this same annoying voice snapped me back to reality.

After all the things I've done, I have the nerve to be jealous and scared. Who is this woman trying to get in between me and my plans? This can't have happened, who was this mystery intruder interfering in our lives?

Automatically I went into detective mode, I have to find out who this mystery caller is. I was going mad tearing through Calvin's drawers, shoe boxes, shoes, sneakers, and found nothing. I went through the closet and in a pair of jeans; I found a receipt from K-Mart.

It read two throw pillows, a microwave and a 25 inch color Television. And there wasn't a damn thing new in this place. No, he's not buying that chick things!

I noticed his laundry bag was gone so he must be at the Laundromat. When he comes in, we've got to talk.

I sat on the bed and looked at the fax machine. I pressed the preview button and the same number showed up about nine times. I said out loud, "Who the hell's number is this?" I called it.

That voice answered. "Hi honey, are you on your way?"

"No, he's not."

"Who, who, who is this," the voice said with a stutter.

"I think you know," I answered, staking my claim.

"How'd you..." I cut her off at the knees.

"How did I get this number? Don't worry about that, are you fucking my husband?"

"Uhm, uhm, I-I-I- think you should talk to your husband."

"No Bitch, I'm talking to you."

"I really think you two need therapy."

"Therapy? He's discussing our business with you?"

"Well, he needed someone to talk to and I was there for him."

While I was on the phone with her, I dialed Calvin on my cell and he answered. I covered the phone so she couldn't hear I was calling him.

"Calvin," I said in a whisper.

"Oh Octavia, you alright? I read about your doctor friend in the paper."

"I need you to come home."

"Are you crying?"

"Please Cal, just come home." I repeated in my calmest voice and hung up turned my attention back to the woman on the other line. I'm trying my damnedest to keep her on the phone so she couldn't call him and warn him.

At the same time I rambled through his junk drawer and in the back of the drawer was a balled up dry rot piece of paper with the name Makini on it and a number in his mother's handwriting.

No, this old bat did not give him his ex-girlfriends new number. I know his mother wanted him with this girl, but to the point of trying to play matchmaker, while he's married to someone else was absolutely disrespectful.

Five minutes later, Calvin comes in the door eager to console me, arm reaching out to me. He said, "Come here Mommy, let Daddy make it better."

"When is the last time you spoke with Makini?"

He stepped back and looked at me and on went the reverse psychology.

"You called me home for that bullshit, these accusations are getting ridiculous?"

"Calvin, I'm going to ask you one more time. When is the last time you spoke with Makini?"

"I haven't spoken to that damn girl in a few years." He looked me right in my eyes and lied, something I've done a million times in the past. I couldn't believe he was so convincing but I have his girlfriend still carrying on the phone.

"Really," I answered, throwing the phone at him. He looked puzzled, put the phone to his ear and put his head down. All I could hear of that conversation was him saying a bunch of "uh huhs" and "okay's" before ending the conversation.

Calvin looked up at me. "Do you want me to leave?"

My heart sank. That's not what I wanted so why was I looking for shit I didn't want to find.

"Calvin, I still love you and I want to make this work."

"You see, Octavia, if it's work then it's hard and I'm tired. Remember our wedding song; *Loving You Is Easier Than Breathing by the Moment*s, Well Tav, I can't breathe at all with you."

"What," I stumbled over my next words trying to choose them carefully. "Are you saying it's over?"

"What I'm saying Octavia is, for at least the last year and a half, you and I have been just going through the motions. You haven't even noticed that I moved out."

"What are talking about, you moved out? There are clothes in the drawers and closets."

"All that shit you bought me, you can keep it." Calvin let me know.

My legs began to shake uncontrollably and the tears began to flow. Calvin got up to walk out the door. I jumped up behind him and grabbed his arm, "I'm not going to let you leave me Calvin," I screamed.

"You can't stop me Tav, let go of me," he growled as he snatched his arm away from me so hard I fell into the glass table. In one swift move, he threw his key on the table. A sudden sense of relief came over him.

"I've been trying to find a way to tell you, but I'm caught now, so fuck it. Besides Octavia, she is about to have my baby in two months, something you couldn't give me."

"But Calvin I- I- want to work this out, I'm pregnant!" I blurted.

"Yeah right," he said with a hint of sarcasm.

"How could you do this to me?"

"Like this." He said as the door slammed behind him. I ran to the door hysterical and screaming.

"Calvin, do not do this." He never missed a step, he kept walking and didn't even turn around but yelled, "I'm out."

He continued. "Oh, I paid the phone bill and you might want to get that cut stitched up. You're bleeding all over the place."

He was right I looked down at my arm and blood was dripping all over the place. I went back in my apartment and stared out the window like a child whose parents just left them at daycare, holding my arm and crying.

***

I began to throw his things down the incinerator talking to myself and cursing out loud with every piece I shoved down the garbage shoot. I lay there in a pile of his coats, clothes, shoes and pictures that I ripped up. Exhausted, numb and bloody, I just laid there.

My arm was beginning to hurt, I thought about poor Stephen and I felt sorry for his daughter. But right now, I think I understand why he jumped, too much all at once.

I went to the emergency room and laid there staring at the ceiling as the Doctor stitched me up and the nurse asked me questions. "Did your husband do this to you, did he hit you?"

I shook my head no, I wished he would have hit me; it would have hurt a helluva lot less.

Chapter 11

The night was sticky and muggy probably from the storm still whipping through the South. My cheeks were beginning to go numb from sitting on the curb. My arm was stitched and wrapped up with gauze. I was sweating like a hog as I picked the petals off the Daisies I brought with me.

A makeshift memorial was placed outside of Stephen's office. There were wilted flowers, half melted candles, cards and handwritten signs saying you'll be missed.

I sat there half the night by myself all cried out. My eyes and lips were puffy, dried white tear stains sat on my cheeks and my hair was desperately in need of a combing. But I didn't care; my life went from heaven to hell in a handbag in less than a week.

I see what drove Stephen to take his own life. It seems as if everything that could go wrong, did. The pain was almost unbearable I thought about joining Stephen. It seemed to be the only way to stop the pain.

But I remember Stephen saying once, "Life has its ups and downs and pain will lessen with each day, time heals all wounds." I guess he stopped believing that himself or that he ran out of patience waiting for the pain to end.

I said my goodbyes to my friend and got back in my SUV. The chill from my air conditioner brought about a frosty shiver in me as my sweat met the cool air. I turned the A/C down and the radio up when my cell vibrated on my hip. I glanced at it and saw 516. For that split second, I hoped it was Lynn telling me he changed his mind or it was just a bad joke. I answered, "Hello."

"What up Tav, its Ron."

I answered in a solemn depressed tone, "Hi, baby boy."

"Heard from Lynn?"

"Nope."

"He hasn't called you?"

"Nope."

"Have you called him?" Ron continued with his line of questioning.

"Nope."

"Octavia! Stop with the one word answers, what's going on with you?"

I laid it on him. Everything came pouring out, the baby, Lynn, Calvin and Stephen's suicide.

"I don't know what's happening to my life Ron, when it rains it pours."

"Damn Oct', your shit is in shambles."

"Thanks for pointing out the obvious."

"Sorry Mami but damn!"

My car began to sputter in the middle of the parkway, eventually it stalled and coasted. I steered it toward the shoulder and finally came to a stop. I ran the A/C for so long that I must have run out of gas.

"SHIT!!!!!" I screamed loud in the phone.

"What happened, you alright?"

I banged my clinched fist over and over again on the steering wheel screaming to the top of lungs like I was having a nervous breakdown. "WHAT DID I EVER DO TO DESERVE THIS? WHAT? WHAT? WHAT?"

Totally forgetting I had dropped the phone and Ron was still holding on. "I'M NOT A BAD PERSON, GOD WHY ME?" I questioned God as a burst of white smoke came from under the hood and the tail pipe. I looked over the hood and the rear view mirror. "OH, THIS IS SOME BULLSHIT!"

I rambled on, "GIMMEE A freakin break."

I reached on the floor retrieved my phone. I could still hear Ron's voice almost in a state of panic, screaming, "Tavia! Octavia! Octavia!" he repeated.

I tried to exhale and take control of myself.

"I'm here Ron," I said in the calmest voice I could muster.

"What happened?"

"I don't know. It's like my truck blew up and white smoke is coming from everywhere."

"You scared me girl," he said, sounding out of breath.

"Sorry, but bullshit is always happening to me."

"Well, you know what they say, bad things tend to happen to good people."

"Well, aren't there other good people some of this bullshit can happen to besides me?"

"Sounds like your engine blew."

"Yeah, that sounds about right. It has to be something like that because bad things keep happening to me."

"How far are you from home?"

"A couple of miles away."

I hadn't given any thought to how I was getting home.

"Call Lynn and tell him to come get you."

"I don't think so."

"Stop being stubborn. Call him; you know he'll pick you up."

"No, I'll walk and call a tow truck from home."

"Walk on the parkway, are you nuts?"

"Well, how else am I going to get there?"

"Call Lynn!!!" Ron insisted.

"Hell no!"

"Tavia, you're as stubborn as a mule, call the man."

"I can't call him. I feel like I'm having a nervous breakdown. I'm going to walk, I need to."

"Don't do that, I'll pick you up."

"By the time you get here, I could be home already."

"Not the way I drive, I'll be there in twenty minutes." Click.

When I took the phone away from my ear, my ear felt wet and I could feel something warm running down my arm. I must have busted my stitches when I beat up on the steering wheel. I looked around my light beige interior. It looked like someone was slaughtered in there, blood was everywhere. I didn't even bother to try to clean it up. I began my walk on the dark deserted parkway talking to myself and swearing, holding my now aching arm.

Twenty-five minutes into my walk, I heard a horn and a male voice yelling out of the window flashing his high beams.

"TAVIA!!!!!!!!"

I hadn't even turned around; the red Mustang pulled up on the shoulder and cut me off, it was Ron.

"Get in!" He demanded.

"You got here from Long Island in record time," I said as I was climbing in his car.

Ron talked and talked. He turned on the interior light and began to wipe off my cheek with a napkin.

"What's that on your face, blood?"

"Oh," I said pulling down the passenger side mirror. "Oh God, I look terrible."

"Yeah you do, there's blood all over your shirt too." He continued to babble on.

I tuned him out looking out the window until he pulled up in my parking lot.

"You gonna be alright, lady?"

"No, I don't think so."

"What do you mean you don't think so? Everything is going to be alright, mark my words."

"I don't know but I don't want to be alone. Can you come up for a little while?"

"I can't, I have to go to work at five."

"Just for a few."

Ron finally agreed.

"Okay but don't let me fall asleep. If I do you gotta get me up at four."

Ron and I sat up talking for hours. I saw he was tired so I left the room to let him get some rest for work.

A few minutes later, I heard Ron calling my name. I went into the bedroom and he was under the covers and talking on the phone.

"Telephone, shorty."

"I didn't hear the phone ring, it better not be Lynn." I warned him.

"Naw, it's your wonder twin, I called her."

"What's up Mi-Mi, we waited for you at Mommy's house." Yvette said.

"I forgot."

"Ron told me what happened. "You alright? Did that nigga hit you?"

"No, he didn't, I'm just a little depressed."

"You need me?"

"No! Ron's here."

"He wants me to come over there."

"For what?"

"To bump uglies."

"To bump uglies," I repeated.

Ron interjected, "Tavia, will you tell her I'm naked under these covers."

I turned around as he lifted the covers, this man is going commando under my sheets. I was instantly uncomfortable.

"Yeah."

"He's butt ass under your covers?"

"Yup."

She's alot like me in that way. We don't like no strange ass man's nakedness all up in our bed, uninvited.

"Well, tell him I had to go. I'll call you tomorrow, love you."

"Love you too."

After I hung up, I got up to walk back into the living room so Ron could get a couple hours of sleep before he went to work. He grabbed the back of my nightgown.

"Lay down," he demanded.

"No, I'm going in the living room so you can sleep." He wouldn't let go of my gown.

"Come on, girl. Lay down, you didn't ask me to keep you company so you can sleep in the other room."

"I know but..."

"But nothing, girl, lay down." He wasn't taking no for an answer.

I reluctantly laid on top of the covers while he laid between them with his heavy arm over my waist. I waited until I heard him snoring and slid out of the bed and went into the living room to go to sleep. I should have learned my lesson years ago with another friend of mine that came to keep me company, when I fell asleep I woke up with his head between my legs.

I wasn't about to let that happen again especially not with Lynn's best friend. I couldn't sleep so I surfed through the channels. I heard Ron rushing off to get to work.

"Why did you get up," he asked, not really waiting for a response rushing towards the door.

"I'll call you later" he said as he bulleted through the door and down the pissy back stairwell.

I'm kind of relieved he was gone. His intentions could have been honorable but I wasn't taking any chances.

Chapter 12

Days and weeks went by. I checked the caller ID every day and not a word from Lynnwood. He must be married by now and Calvin must be a father by now too.

The more days that go by, the madder I get.

It's just me and my growing belly. How did my life end up such a mess with not a daddy in sight?

I've been seriously considering terminating this pregnancy because the more I think about my situation the more I realize I can't do this. I called Ron.

"Ron, I need you."

"What's up, lady? I haven't heard from you in weeks. I've tried to call you and I even came over the bridge, are you ok? How's my godchild?"

"I decided that I want to have an abortion."

"Tavia, don't don't ..."

Before he could finish, I cut him off.

"Please don't say anything except I'll go with you, because I'm afraid I'll lose my nerve."

"But Octavia listen, if you just call Lynn..."

I cut him off again.

"If I just call Lynn, what? He'll decide his marriage is a mistake, huh? Well, I don't want him like that if I can't be number one now; I refuse to be number two."

"I'm telling you girl, he has a right to know either way."

"You know what Ron, Lynn's got the right to know dick! You're under the wild misconception I give a flying fuck what Lynn thinks right now. I was growing impatient. Forget it."

Click.

I hung up. I didn't want to hear anything, Lynn didn't deserve shit. Before I could put the phone down it rang again, I didn't have to look at the caller ID I already knew it was Ron.

"WHAT Ron," I answered.

"Octavia, don't hang up, listen to me. I'll go with you. I just want to make sure you're sure about this decision. You're not in a proper state of mind right now; you have a lot going on in your life. I just don't want you to regret your choice."

Ron was right. I couldn't grasp a clear thought, my heart was broken, I was lonely and depressed. Not to mention the fact that I felt like a fool, it all was too overwhelming.

I cut myself off from everyone in my life. I haven't answered my door or my phones. I haven't even been to work in weeks. I've been walking around my apartment in the dark in my shaggy old bathrobe and fuzzy slippers. I couldn't hide this baby any longer. I'm starting to show.

"So when are you going to the Clinic?"

"I'm going to call when I get off the phone with you, they will probably tell me to come in on Friday."

"Well when you get the exact time and day text me and let me know, okay? I'm on my way to my second job; if you need me don't hesitate to call."

"Thank you, Ron."

"No problem, baby girl."

We hung up and I searched through the yellow pages and found the number I was searching for. And just like I thought, they said Friday at nine A.M. I text messaged Ron.

FRIDAY NINE A.M. WHITE PLAINS, the text read.

Five minutes later, I received a text back.

SEE YOU THEN, the text read.

I 'm not sure how I feel about my decision yet, but I gotta do it.

It was Friday morning seven A.M., the rays from the sun kissed me peeking through my downward pointing blinds. I felt as if I had just closed my eyes. I struggled with my conscience all week and I wrestled with my decision all night, so sleep didn't come easy. I lay there wallowing in self-pity unable to muster a tear, wishing my life could have gone in another direction.

I fell to my knees and prayed.

Dear Lord, please forgive me for this horrible sin I'm about to commit. God, I don't see any other way right now, point me in the way you would have me go. I know what I'm about to do is wrong and what a thing to ask, please give me the strength I need.

Bling, Bling, pause Bling, Bling.

Just then, my pleas were interrupted by the sound of my door bell.

I answered it and pressed nine to buzz the door, I knew it had to be Ron. I saw no need to ask who it was.

I looked at the clock and realized he was a little early so I better take a quick shower. I ran and unlocked the door and trotted back to the bathroom and jumped in the shower. I heard the door open and yelled out.

"I'll be out in a sec," I shut the door and locked it. I didn't want him venturing in here. I didn't want a repeat performance of an uncomfortable situation between me and him.

I showered in a hurry because I didn't want to leave Ron waiting too long. I stepped my foot out of the shower, opened the door and I could see feet next to my bed.

What the hell was he doing in my room, I asked myself, than repeated my comment out loud as I stepped in my room half covered up in a towel. Just as I went into flip mode, I realized it was Lynn sitting there on my bed.

"What the hell," I spat out as I clinched the top of my towel to keep it from falling.

"Hello to you too," he responded in a voice that melted me like butter. He reached around my waist under my towel and pulled me close to him, wrapped his arms around me tightly and laid his head on my damp plump belly and squeezed. My hands still clutching my towel I managed to muster up some words.

"What are you doing here?"

"I had to see you."

Now what part of the game was this? I was confused. I pulled away and inconspicuously trying to cover my growing belly with my hands and towel. He pulled me near and rested his ear on my stomach and rubbed my thigh with his hand. He sat back and said, "You look beautiful, you're glowing."

My knees abandoned me; his voice was so sincere and loving.

"Why didn't you tell me?" He moved his hand from my thigh to my now quivering belly.

"Tell you what," I replied, playing dumb.

"Octavia really, do we have to go there today, why didn't you tell me about our child?"

"Because, I paused and continued, "the only thing you wanted to hear was guess what I did today."

"Yeah, I did say that didn't I," almost sounding ashamed of himself. "But baby, I didn't mean it. You should have talked it over with me."

Lynn kissed my sweet belly button and around it, all across my belly and felt around my aching breast softly kissing around my pubic area. He inhaled deep breaths taking in the scent of my snack box.

"Mmmmmmmm, I love the way you smell," he confessed with a smile as smell was a fond memory. He kept touching and caressing, I felt like I was on fire.

He felt so good touching me, I missed him. Lynn tugged at my towel until I reluctantly let it go and it hit the floor.

"I missed you baby," he whispered.

I melted in his grip; he never got up from the bed. He turned my body with his hands, kissing me around my waist and my backside, wrapping his arms around my waist once again rubbing my stomach from behind. With my five pound heavier ass in his face, Lynn kissed my crack and tongued it as he bent me over. I wanted to tell him no! But my body wouldn't let me and I know my heart would have never forgiven me.

I love him still. No matter how hard I tried to hate him, he owned my heart. And apparently my body too, I surrendered myself to his kisses. All the fight was kissed out of me by his soft sweet lips.

"I missed you so much." I just let go and let Lynn in.

This must be God answering my prayer; happiness fell on me like a warm rain. Things are going to work out after all, Ron was right. I should have told him and I wouldn't have had to suffer so long. I shut my eyes and opened my legs, as well my revived heart to Lynn. As he went straight for the backdoor, my body was ready for him and it was damn near poetic. He slayed me and he knew it.

"I love you, Octavia," he repeated just as he reached climax. He pulled out of my backside and covered my back and bottom with his unsuccessful egg seeking sprinters.

We lay there with my back pressed firmly against his stomach practically stuck together from sweat and cum. His soldier resting in my cheeks, he held my hands in his. I looked at his hand and noticed the tan line from where a ring once sat. *Is their marriage over?* I thought, getting happy. I questioned him.

"Lynn, what are you doing here," I reluctantly asked.

"I spoke with Ron and he told me you were pregnant and what you planned to do today."

"Lynn, I just wanted us to..."

Before I could finish, he cut me off and cut off my happiness.

"I'm glad you made the right choice because neither one of us are in a position to have a kid right now."

"What!!!" I shouted as I jumped up from the cum stained bed. "What are you doing here if it wasn't to make things right?"

"I wanted to make sure you got there okay, and things will be right when this is done, we'll be back to normal."

This self-righteous son of a bitch! He just showed up to make sure I got rid of it and got some bonus butt for his trouble.

"Let me hurry up and get re-showered and dressed so I can get *your* life back to normal."

"Come on Tavia, don't be like that you're over reacting."

"Over reacting my ass," I shouted. I just threw up my hand and shut the bathroom door, talking to myself loud enough for him to hear.

"Me and my dumb ass thinking with my coochie, I can't believe I'm hung up on this fuckin prick. You're so stupid, stupid, stupid," I scolded myself. "Everyone has that someone they're a fool for, he must be my someone."

I got dressed in a hurry, not saying a word and walked to the door. He followed. I opened the door, stuck the key in the lock and stood there tapping my foot. He walked past me expressionless. The ride to the chop shop was uneasy and tension filled.

***

The waiting area was packed; about a dozen and a half females of all ages, sizes and ethnic backgrounds waiting for their turn to get a life sucked out of them. Some were there with their mother's, girlfriends, unwanted baby daddies and friends. And here I sit with another woman's husband.

I sat there filling out my questionnaire with Lynn looking over my shoulder.

A few minutes later, my name was called. I got up to go talk to the business receptionist, Lynn followed. She explained the cost with anesthesia would be fifty dollars more than without. "But your insurance will cover it; you could either get the abortion pill or the procedure."

I asked curiously, "What is the Pill about?"

"Well you take the pill here in our office and in 24 to 48 hours you should miscarry at home."

Lynn interjected pulling out the four hundred and fifty dollars, "She'll do the procedure."

The pill seemed too risky anyway but how dare this man make decisions for my body. "Do you want to hop up on the table with me to make sure it's done," I said in an angry tone. Lynn didn't say a word; the receptionist wrote up a receipt and told us to have a seat. Lynn tore up the receipt and threw it in the garbage before we could get out of her office.

"Trying not to leave a paper trail, huh?"

"You know how I feel about paperwork."

"No! But I'm beginning to know how you feel about me."

Again Lynn said nothing, he just sat there and took my ridicule as he should. He deserves it. Once again, I heard my name.

I got up to go through the door when I heard a voice say, "Sorry sir, you're not allowed back here, you have to wait here."

Lynn almost looked disappointed. The tall light skinned nurse shut the door in Lynn's face and ushered me to a blood drawing room and then to the ultrasound room, where a short dark-skinned lady sat with what looked like a giant dildo with a condom on it in her hands.

"Take off your clothes and put on a gown. When you're done, lie here on the table and put your feet in the stirrups." I obediently did as I was told and she inserted the dildo look alike up into my vagina as she watched on the monitor.

"Can you tell the sex," I asked.

She said nothing.

"Can I look at the screen?"

She looked over at me over her metal rimmed frames.

"Are you sure," she asked, turning the screen in my direction.

There it was, my son or daughter in its first and last cameo.

She pointed out its little arms and legs and its awkward shaped head, which she swore was normal for a fetus this age. A knock on the door interrupted our session.

"Peggy," the voice said, "are you done?"

"Just finishing up," she answered. She told me to go next door to the consultation room and have a seat.

"Are you all right, Miss," the woman behind the desk asked.

"No," I answered. "I really don't want to do this," I admitted as the image of my unborn innocent child danced in my head.

"You don't have to," the woman said no one is forcing you to. "You can change your mind at any time."

"No, I have to; let's just get it over with."

She walked me to a waiting area where women sat like sheep at the slaughter house waiting for their turn. We all looked nervous and scared with the exception of one or two repeat abortion veterans telling us all, "Oh girl you'll be in and out before you know it, when you wake up it will be over and you can go on with your life."

Shit they make it sound like their pregnancy was a burden from hell and this baby was interfering with the plans. Talk about girls interrupted. These women must work for the devil himself or for the clinic. She pitched abortion to us like she was selling an old used car.

With every name called it was getting closer and closer to my date with destiny. Just when I thought that tear well, was all dried up, it sprang a leak and the tears began to flow, it was my turn.

I couldn't stop crying I went into an operating room that was freezing where everyone was already wearing their masks like they were hiding their faces. Just like the executioners did in medieval times. Tears were streaming down the sides of my face as I tucked the sheet underneath my shivering body.

A masked person with the voice of an angel rubbed my head and whispered, "Everything is going to be okay. Take a deep breath and count backwards from one hundred."

I felt myself dozing and I began to plead, "No please, No, I changed my mind trying to pull myself up off the table."

The last thing I remember was the image of the ultrasound in my head. I thought, *Lord forgive me!* I could no longer hold on to consciousness.

***

I don't remember having a dream or even a thought since my plea for forgiveness, I was woken up very abruptly, by a young girl who looked like she was straight out of high school.

"Wake up honey," she said. I didn't even realize I was out. I was trying to pull it together as I looked around the recovery room to a bunch of sad faces sitting up in lounge chairs eating cookies, drinking orange juice and fighting back tears.

Once again we were called one by one into a little office where a nurse sat giving out Tylenol and antibiotics.

I felt like I was asleep for hours but in actuality, it was only out about 15 minutes. They let me sit for about five more minutes when my name was called.

"Come in and shut the door."

I did again as I was told. I sat down and waited for my Tylenol and antibiotics.

"Octavia, how do you feel?"

I was having a little trouble shaking off the anesthesia and my head was swimming. I felt guilty but what's done is done now.

"I'm a little woozy."

"It will pass," she said, handing me a piece of paper and a pen. "Please read this paper and sign it."

My vision was a little blurry.

"I can't read the paper," I told her. "Can you just tell me what it says and show me where to sign?"

"It says that you refused the procedure and you decided not to terminate your pregnancy."

"What, you didn't do it?" I exclaimed.

"You asked us not to as you were going under so the Doctor thought it would be best that he not perform the abortion."

"Thank you, Thank you," I repeated jumping up to go change but the woozy head knocked me back to my seat.

"Take your time, Miss."

I got up and tried it again. I walked to the room to put my clothes back on. All the time thinking, *what I'm I going to tell Lynn? I'm not going to tell Lynn a damn thing.*

Chapter 13

I walked out of the back office with the image of my unborn child in my head and laid eyes on Lynn pacing. He was wearing a hole in the floor. My face owned no expression.

"Everything done," he asked obviously concerned about himself, the anger was building in me. I didn't answer.

"Are you okay," he asked.

I couldn't hold my peace. "That should have been the first thing you asked me when I came out of there." The waiting area got quiet; the room sat on pins and needles waiting for my next word.

"Okay Tavia," he whispered. "Lower your voice."

"Lower *my* voice? No, you lower your motherfuckin voice. I don't care what these people think about me. I don't even care what you think anymore. You're a dick, all you're concerned about is Lynn and what's best for Lynn and Lynn's situation."

"Shhhhhhh," he said, firmly gripping my arm and ushering me toward the exit.

"No you didn't just try to shush me." I bounced back, snatching my arm from his grasp.

As soon as we got out the door, Lynn grabbed me by both shoulders and pushed me against the wall.

"Ok, Ok Octavia. I get it, I'm sorry," he said never opening his teeth.

I just broke down and cried in his arms as he wrapped his arms around me and held me. "I'm sorry, I'm sorry," he repeated. "If the situation was different we could..."

I didn't let him finish. I snatched away, composing myself because I was still feeling a little woozy. I got in the car and put my head back. Lynn lagged behind like a child in trouble. I watched him walk around the front of the car and answer his phone.

He reached in his pocket for his keys and when he pulled out the keys something else fell out of his pocket with them. It hit the ground and rolled down the parking lot and came to a stop at the curb. It was his wedding band. He had secretly tucked it away in his pocket, in a feeble attempt to hide it from me.

I started to draw his attention to his never ending band of trust that fell out of his pocket. When I realized what it was, I didn't say a word. Let him explain where his wedding ring is when he gets home. He sat down and put his fingers to his lips signaling me to keep quiet.

"Oh Hell no, you didn't just shush me again."

He reached over and put his hand over my mouth. It has to be Nadia. I'll show his black ass. I continued to talk through his hand trying to pry his fingers one by one off my lips with my hands. He removed his hand, covered the mouth of the phone and begged me.

"Please Octavia, just five minutes," and continued on with his conversation. And I continued on with my ranting. With his hand back over my mouth, I bit him to free myself.

"Ouch," he blurted. Nadia must have asked what happened, while shaking the pain off his hand he answered, "I slammed my foot in the door."

He cut his eyes at me. The eyes I once saw my life in were looking at me with such anger.

That was it. I waited until he got to the next light and jumped out the car and hailed a cab. The cab pulled up in my parking lot and Lynn's car was sitting there, waiting. I hopped out and double timed it to the building with Lynn right on my heels. "Octavia, can I talk to you?"

I ignored him and kept it moving. I got to my apartment door and there was a piece of paper taped to it. I snatched it off, unlocked my door and slammed it in Lynn's face. He knocked; I could hear his voice from outside the door.

"Stop being like that."

I didn't answer.

"Are you going to answer me?"

"I ain't answering shit," I said to myself.

"I'll call you later."

I still didn't answer, the hallway got silent. I sat on the sofa rubbing my stomach and began to open a letter from the City Marshall's office.

What the hell is this, I thought? A notice to evict, WHAT! The letter stated that I had 48 hours to vacate the premises.

"Oh my God, why?"

I read on, it said due to nonpayment of rent. Calvin always paid the rent so how could they say it wasn't paid? I jumped on the phone, called the number on the eviction notice and a woman voice answered, "Good afternoon, Clay Thomas Williams, how may I direct your call?"

I explained my situation to the pleasant voice on the phone, she politely listened and then said, "Sorry there's nothing we can do for you, we've been sending you court summons for almost six months and you were a no show at each one."

"Your case went to court again six weeks ago and a decision was made on the behalf of the housing authority, and you have exactly 48 hours to remove your belongs from the unit or the City Marshall will throw your things in the street."

"How much do I owe?"

"The amount of back rent owed is twelve thousand dollars."

"Twelve thousand? What? That would mean I haven't paid rent in almost a year."

"Yes, about eight months is right."

"What if I give you the money now?"

"You see, at this point, there's nothing that can be done. They don't even want your money, now they just want you out."

"Is there anyone I can speak to? I'm about to have a baby. I need some place to live."

"I'm sorry, there's nothing that can be done. Have a good day."

I was stunned and confused. I called Calvin's cell only to find that his number was changed. I called his job, he no longer works there.

I just took a seat where I was standing in the middle of the floor. I didn't have a plan. I called my sister at my mother's house. I explained to her what was going on. She tried to help me come up with solutions, but there were none.

"Octavia, you can come live with me. I know you like having your own but what's mine is yours and Mommy says bring yourself and your things over to her house. She'll take care of you."

"I know, but I can't live with Mommy. I will take you up on your offer, just for a few months until I can find a place. Thanks, Mi-Mi."

"I love you girl, do you need me to bring anything?"

"Just boxes, I only have forty-eight hours to get out."

"All right, I'll grab Omar and some of his friends and start your packing."

I didn't have time to assess the situation and exactly what was going on. Calvin took care of the rent and the phone bill. I called the U-Haul company to reserve a truck for the next day, I gave them my debit MasterCard number, they ran it and told me I had insufficient funds to rent this truck.

"There must be some mistake," I told the gentleman on the other end of the line. "Can you run it again? I know I have five thousand dollars in my checking account." The male voice came back to the phone and said, "I'm sorry, Miss. I tried twice. Maybe you should call your bank."

"Thank you," I politely replied. I hung up and called the bank.

The voice on the phone at the bank informed me of a large check I wrote for five thousand dollars to Maryland State Financial Mortgage Company for the down payment on a house.

"House? I didn't give a down payment for a house to anyone." Then I thought, I hung up the phone and went directly to Calvin's filing cabinet which was always locked. I took a steak knife and pried the drawer open. I found several receipts for furniture, a microwave and a mattress.

It took my mind back to when I found that receipt in Calvin's pocket and he tried to convince me he and an old friend got in the same line at K-mart. She paid for his stuff on her credit card and he gave her the cash for it.

I continued to search and found about six court summons and notices to vacate the premises. And the paper that beat it all, a loan application for a house in Maryland.

All those receipts for furniture were for him. Forget sharing a place in line, he was furnishing and putting a down payment on a house with my fuckin' money.

The checkbook was gone but what could I do, he's still my husband and he can take money from the account without any questions asked. I should have changed the account when he left but I was so caught up in what was going on at the time, I didn't think about it. I continued to search through his file cabinet.

I don't know what I was looking for now, I knew all I needed to.

I stumbled across an envelope full of pictures of Calvin and Makini in my apartment, pictures of them with his mother in Virginia, even pictures at her first GYN appointment, and the last picture was of them two together in front of a house holding a sign that said SOLD on it.

I closed the envelope. Taped to the back of the envelope was an ultrasound picture, addressed to me. On the back, it said:

To Octavia: These are pictures of a life you'll never have.

Normally, I would have been shattered but I'm numb. I put the pictures back in the file cabinet, closed it and started packing.

***

Yvette and I packed all through the night and the next day.

My brother Omar and his friends loaded my belongings, my memories and my life, piece by piece into the U-Haul my mother rented me.

There was one item left in the apartment when the Marshall came just like she said they would.

"What about the file cabinet," my sister asked.

"It's garbage."

"What about it, what's in it?"

"That's garbage, let the Marshall throw it out."

I walked out as the City Marshall was changing the locks and putting a yellow notice on the door that told anyone that would read it; *These premises were vacated by the City Marshal's Of the New Rochelle City Court. Any entry to these premises by any individual is punishable by law.*

My brother Omar drove my memories to storage.

Yvette asked, "Did you turn off the phone?"

"Check."

"Did you call and have the cable turned off?"

"Check."

"Did you call and have your mail held at the post office?"

"Now *that* I forgot to do. Come to think of it, let me check the mail before we go."

I checked the mail and there was one letter in the box. It was from The White Plains Planned Parent Hood. *What the hell could this be*, I thought to myself, as I was tearing open my letter. As I walked out of my apartment and life that I once knew, my nosey neighbors were sitting on benches, hanging out the windows to watch my walk of shame.

I jumped in the passenger seat of my sister's car and we began to drive off. I realized it was a check and a letter explaining the reason for the four hundred dollar refund, minus fifty dollars for the anesthesia, for refusal of service. I forgot all about that money. I'm going to take the money and put it away in our child's savings account. At least he'll have something from his father.

Fast forward

More than a year had passed. I sold three songs to various artists that were number one on the charts for ten weeks straight. I even did a movie score and soundtrack, all my heartache has made me a hell of a writer.

My finances were back in order. I purchased a two bedroom apartment in Battery Park City and my son is almost six months old. He's the spitting image of his father.

My life was back on track.

Gabriel and I turned in early one night and my phone rang around one o'clock am. It startled me so badly that I jumped out of the bed, answered the remote, and got my son's bottle; until I finally answered the phone.

Gabriel was churning, the phone disturbed his sleep. "Whoever this is, it better be good, you woke up my son. Hello! Hello!" I spoke into the phone.

There was silence, no one was there, must have been a wrong number. I took the phone off the hook and laid back down. My heart was pounding from the phone ringing and scaring me out of my slumber. I rocked Gabriel back to sleep and finally dozed off again. I heard a knock on my door, it could only be the doorman, so I opened it without peeking through the peep hole and there stood Lynn.

"How did you find me," I asked, trying to slam the door. Lynn put his foot in it to hold it open.

"I have my ways."

"How did you get past the doorman?"

"He was preoccupied so I slipped by him."

"Please leave." I felt anger building up inside of me.

"Tavia, before you say anything else, let me just say I'm sorry for everything and I love you."

"You know love makes you do strange things, I told Nadia everything even about the baby and I left her. I've spent more than a year searching for you, now that I found you, I don't ever want to let you go."

He backed me up against the wall and the door slammed behind him. He hugged me. "I missed you baby, I was just scared, that's all."

"Lynn, I was scared too, and how did you find out about the baby?"

"Ron said he spoke to you one day and he heard a baby crying in the background but you denied having one. I didn't know for sure until I called and you answered the phone and said, "This better be good, you woke up my son."

"Can I see my son?"

"You don't deserve to see him, you didn't want him."

"Just let me be a part of his life, if you don't want me anymore I understand but don't shut me out of his life. I'm going to make it up to you and him, you'll see, just let me."

He was chipping away at that ice wall I built around my heart and I gave in and let him see his son.

I walked him to the bedroom where our son slept. He picked Gabriel up embraced him and cried. "I'm glad you kept him, I really am.

He looks just like me," he choked with emotion filled words.

"Yes he does," I echoed.

As Lynn embraced his new found responsibility, he rubbed Gabriel's head with the same hand I tried to bite off more than a year ago. The teeth marks I left on his hand proved to be a constant reminder of me.

One year and a half has gone by and we're married and I'm pregnant with our second child, Octavia.

Octavia Michaels had everything she could ever want out of love but it took two men to give it to her. She lied, she cheated, and she gambled on love and lost.

Octavia's lies and deceit ruined lives and wrecked homes including her own.

And then there were none.

Coming soon...by Clay Thomas Williams

The Deacons Daughter (un-edited)

Chapter 1

A loud roaring noise outside my bedroom window wakes me from a dead sleep. I jumped and damn near fell out of the bed but the metal hand cuffs still attached to my wrist kept my upper body from following my legs.

A night stick, k-y jelly and several empty condom wrappers clutter my night stand. The taste of my sins were evident from the night before still radiating from my mouth and the smell of Grey Goose seeping through my pores from my sweaty lust filled night of drinking. I squinted my cold filled eyes to see the alarm clock posted across the room on top of my television; the bright red numbers read nine fifty- five. Oh shit, I over slept. Let me hustle. I reached in my nightstand drawer and retrieved a spare set of hand cuff keys and un cuffed me.

I laid my head back on the pillow just for a second to regroup and give myself that, get up Angela you can do it speech. I realized my co sinner from the night before was still there. Damn, I must have had too much to drink. I'm still feeling a little inebriated.

I usually put him out before sun rises like a vampire. He's still sleeping like a baby that just finished suckling from his mama's breast. He's so damn sexy and that early morning pee hard is raising my sheets like a teepee getting me in the mood for some bad breath, still half-drunk mushy marinated sex. Let me wake Dirk Diggler for an early morning romping.

"Officer Pickett wake up we overslept, and I've got to get running."

"Good morning girl." Before he even opened those chestnut eyes, "What time is it?"

"It's about nine-fifty something. Don't you have to work or something, someone to arrest, put in jail or something?

"Nope."

Well lucky him, he still has to go, he don't have to go home, but he's got to get the hell up out of here.

Officer Hassan Pickett is one of my best customers. He's a real anal man. I think he's catching feelings so I'm going to have to stop taking dates with him. He reached over and grabbed my perfectly round ass to pull me on top of him as his butter soft hands searched my body as if I were hiding some concealed weapon. He was performing a very thorough search, I could feel his teepee riser tapping me on the crack of my ass in-between my legs. I planted my lips close to his ear and whispered, "Let me help you put that condom on."

Officer Pickett reached over to the night stand franticly fumbling around for the box of Trojans shaking it to find it was empty.

"It's done Ma, he said in that sweet West Indian accent."

"Done? What do you mean it's done," mimicking his accent?

"There's no more Ma."

"Damn, oh well then, I guess I'll get up and start my day."

"Well, I've known you for a few years, I can trust you right?"

"You must have bumped your damn head on the head board last night; I don't know you like that. No glove no love, see ya."

I jumped out of my king size bed and headed for the shower.

Grabbing my towel off the bedroom door and shouted, "Let yourself out through the bathroom door. This mu'fucka must have lost his damn mind, no condom ha! He must be crazy, I mumbled to myself. I see this dude once every few weeks, yeah I've known him for about four almost five years, I don't know him like that. He's only a trick.

A tap on the bathroom door disturbed my shower.

"Yes, Officer Pickett," I yelled through the door.

"Just wanted you to know I was out, and why can't you call me Hassan."

"Because, its business boo, and you're a client."

The bathroom door opened and I heard his humble voice.

"Angel, I think you should get out of this life and we can be together."

"Oh you think that huh? Well Officer Pickett, I responded without even opening the shower curtain. I think you should leave now."

"Angel, I'll take care of you, you don't have to live this way."

"You already take care of me, you're my best client and I live this way because I choose to."

Why do people think just because you sell ass you're stupid? I've got a Doctoral Degree in Clinical Therapy, along with two Bachelor Degrees in Child Psychology and a Master Degree in Sexual Psychology. The sex business paid my way through college and pays for this lavish lifestyle. It allows me to live in this luxury apartment in Trump's Towers overlooking the Hudson and I have a Porsche truck parked downstairs. I'm fine with the what's and the hows.

I listened for Officer Pickett as I stepped out of the shower, I peeked out the door into my bedroom to see if he was still sitting in my room but he was gone. My bed was made neatly with hospital corners so tight I could bounce a quarter on it. There was an envelope on the pillow. As I dried off, I fingered through the money in the envelop thirty five hundred for the entire night. I don't know how he affords me on a cop's salary; he must be doing more than protecting and serving. But hey, it's not my business how he gets it as long as I get it. It's all there; I put the envelope in the nightstand drawer with the others from other clients that I save until the first of the month for deposit.

Officer Pickett is the only trick I bring to my home; I've known him for almost five years. He lives and works in Jersey, just over the George Washington Bridge. I usually only see him once every two months. Lately, I've been seeing him more. Again, I don't know where he gets the money on a cop's salary, but I don't ask as long as he keeps contributing to the Angela loves to live well fund.

The sex isn't half bad so I don't mind breaking him off every now and again, but it's just a job and he still has to pay. I learned years ago sex and money go together and the men I deal with learned that little bit of information from day one. YOU must invest to undress and I have been told I was addictive. I always tell them, if you want to play you've got to pay and I'm an expensive habit.

I don't waste time with people that have nine to fives; only real money makers spark my attention and most of my clients are men of power. I never do anything strange for a little piece of change.

Officer Pickett is different. I met him during my junior year of college when I was coming home from spring break. I usually leave my car parked at Newark Airport, when my plane lands I can just drive on home. I hit the jersey turnpike, driving a little over the speed limit when I saw lights in my review and a voice telling me to pull over. "Fuck," I yelled as I pulled over, I could see a tall brown figure in uniform walking towards my car.

"Ma' am do you have any idea how fast you were going?"

"As a matter of fact Officer I do, somewhere in the neighborhood of 80 mph."

"Do you realize you could have killed someone or yourself?"

Well no disrespect Officer Pickett, I said squinting my eyes to read his name tag but that was not my intention. I have to pee, and I do apologize. However, you're not gonna give me a ticket AND a lecture.

"Feisty lil thing aren't you."

"Sir really, I just got in from Puerto Rico and I was just trying to get home, but I do have to pee very badly. I may have to get out and go on the side of the road if you don't hurry up."

"Then I'll have to give you a ticket for public lewdness."

"Well Officer Pickett," I started removing myself from the car pulling my skirt up and squatting on the side of the highway and relieved myself.

"Just give me that ticket too. Do you have any Kleenex?" I asked.

Without saying a word Officer Pickett walked over to his patrol car, dug around and walked back to where I was squatting, shaking his head laughing and handed me some Kleenex.

"Thanks Officer, you do protect and serve."

"You're pushing it young lady," he said as he was walked back to his vehicle and sat there.

I fixed my clothes and walked back to my car and waited on my tickets. Fifteen or more minutes have passed, so I laid my head back and closed my eyes, feeling a little jet lagged. A few moments' later Officer Pickett walks back over to my window and tapped on the glass.

"What, are you taking a nap?"

"Seriously Officer, it's been like a half an hour and I'm tired as all hell."

"I guess you really had to go huh?"

"Look Officer, I admitted I was wrong and my only defense is I had to pee. So can I get my ticket so I can go?"

Officer Pickett looked at me and smiled, handed me my information back along with a business card with his information on it and said, "Drive safely, you want to get back to New Ro in one piece don't you?"

"I sure do," I responded throwing the paperwork he handed me into my passenger seat as I put my car in drive. I drove the speed limit until I exited the GWB into NYC; from there I made it to New Rochelle and into my father's driveway in less than 20 minutes. I gathered my papers and bag from the front passenger seat and dragged my tired body up to my bedroom, kicked my shoes off and stretched out across my neatly tucked comforter.

Coming Soon from Tanya Robinson

Dangerous Desires (un-edited)

Max

I watched her from a distance as she got closer to the double doors that would eventually bring us face to face. This one was smooth as silk; I could tell that quickly. She glided through the doors in an effortless strut like Olivia Pope without the stomping. She stopped for a moment as she surveyed the area. She looked at the two windows that read registration and a third window that said triage area. She adjusted her body and headed to the reception area where a Triage Nurse motioned her to come in. Hell, for all I knew she could have been coming in for an STD. I didn't even care for a split second because my little Mister was telling me something different at the time. Me and him had to get up close and personal with her. I don't know why I kept staring at this particular one. It was something about her. It was part arousal and part intrigue. I see women come and go all day when I choose to fill in for a no-show. Shamar Thornton, my employee who was supposed to be here, had a dental appointment. I told him I would pick up his slack until he returned. I could have easily sent someone else, but I had to go downtown later so it wasn't an issue. I didn't mind, besides, I always manage to pick up something at the hospital while I'm here anyway. I decided that Silk was going to be just that. Her instincts must have kicked in and she sensed someone was staring at her. She turns her head my way. And what do I do, I turned my head as fast as I could like a sucker would. What is up with that? How a man like me get punked by a chick like that. Doesn't she know who I am? I must be tripping.

I believe in lust at first sight, hit it at first sight, and after that last nut, outta sight.

Michelle, the triage nurse gave her a 'hey girl' hug and if I read her lips correctly they said "Are you nauseous? Damn, was she pregnant? Was she suffering from morning sickness? I ain't gon mess with no pregnant chick. Although I'm an equal opportunity lover, even I'm not doing that. It's a line I wouldn't cross. To my knowledge I haven't thus far, but who knows as he began humming Chris Brown's song "These girls ain't loyal."

My eyes watched intently as I tried to make out her lip movements. No, don't turn your head I silently voiced. I won't be able to see your mouth speak to me to tell me what I need to know. It looks like she's entering her information. What was she entering though? Chelle's my girl; I have no doubt that she will give a brother an assist. I had to avert my eyes because a young lady that was waiting to be seen started talking too loud on her cell phone. I walked over to her and said "Miss if you want to talk on your phone, you're going to have to go outside the door and finish your call."

"I've been here for over an hour and I haven't been seen yet."

"Miss, you know you are seen in order of severity, not by the time you walk through the doors to register."

"Who are you, one of the hospital suits from upstairs? Y'all need to do something about this."

"No, I'm head of security.

"Where's your uniform then?"

"I don't need one."

"Why not?"

"Because, I just don't." *If this chick don't quit it with the twenty damn questions.* I turn to look back at Silk, she was gone.

"Well, where is the security officer that is usually here."

"Look, I hope you get called soon, I have to get back to the desk."

I started walking back to the desk then stopped and walked into the triage reception office. Hey Chelle, what it do?

"What can I do for you Mr. Knight? As a matter of fact the answer is no."

"Whoa, wait a minute what did I do? "You don't even know if I was going to ask you for anything."

"Yes, I do," she says as she taps her pen on the desk.

"Ah, my feelings are hurt," as he places his hand on his heart.

"What do you want Max?

"Okay, you got me. Guilty as charged. The woman that was just in here, you know her, y'all looked kinda friendly. What's the deal with her?"

"Yes, and it's none of your business."

"Oh it's like that now. I thought we was kool and the gang."

"We are and you're not her type okay."

"How do you know?"

"Cause she's my Soror and my sons Godmommy, that's why."

"Ohhhhhh, so you do know her. I ask excitedly. Is she pregnant?"

"No, why would you ask that?

"Because it looked liked you asked if she was nauseous."

"Look, you take your lip reading ass out of my office. She's off limits. You hear me."

I put up my hands to her showing her my palms and walk back to the desk. Hmmmm, I know I really want her now as a wicked smile covered my face. Game on Silk.

www.ingramcontent.com/pod-product-compliance
Lightning Source LLC
Chambersburg PA
CBHW051825170626
46807CB00003B/1028